JUST ANOTHER ANGEL

Angel's debut escapade?

In the exciting but sometimes dangerous London of the 1980s, Fitzroy Maclean Angel, jazz trumpet player and illegal taxi driver, meets a beautiful and enigmatic blonde – and that's just the start of his troubles. Hotly pursued by a jail-bird gangster and his thuggish henchman, a maverick cop bent on revenge, and a dogged Inland Revenue inspector, he finds his life becoming more complicated by the minute. And just how an emerald pendant, a woman's peace camp and a wad of French francs fit into the picture, he can hardly imagine...

JUST ANOTHER ANGEL

JUST ANOTHER ANGEL

by

Mike Ripley

Magna Large Print Books
Long Preston, North Yorkshire,
BD23 4ND, England.

British Library Cataloguing in Publication Data.

Ripley, Mike
    Just another Angel.

    A catalogue record of this book is
    available from the British Library

    ISBN   978-0-7505-2759-0

First published in Great Britain 1988 by Collins

Copyright © 1988, 2006 Mike Ripley

Cover illustration by arrangement with
Telos Publishing

The moral right of the author has been asserted

Published in Large Print 2008 by arrangement with
Telos Publishing Ltd.

Magna Large Print is an imprint of Library Magna Books Ltd.

Printed and bound in Great Britain by
T.J. (International) Ltd., Cornwall, PL28 8RW

For three women:
Alyson, who never doubted,
Beth and Ada Sylvia.

And two men:
John Grant and Gwyn Lawrence,
who inspired in very different ways.

CHAPTER ONE

I was in the Gun having the first drink of the day, or the last drink of the night before, depending on how you looked at it, when she came through the door with a bunch of Hooray Henries six feet deep and twice as thick.

The Gun, I'd better explain, is that rarity in England: a pub that opens when the punters want it to. Situated an apple-core throw away from Spitalfields fruit and veg market behind Liverpool Street station, the Gun has a special dispensation to open at six in the morning to serve all bona-fide market traders. Not that Trippy and Dod and I were bona-fide marketeers – most of the real ones have pretty dubious fides – but I'd done the landlord a favour or three in the past and was known there. Which is what it's all about, really, isn't it?

The reason we were there at 6.30 am was the gig in Brighton the night before. The venue had turned out to be a private club and a gay bar to boot. We had innocently thought that the Queen's Head would be a pub. Not that that was the problem. We had arrived late to find two other members of the band had turned up and gone again when they saw the clientele, and two had simply not turned up at all. Add to that a failed amplifier, which meant the club's disco was out of action, and the club owner was about to have his hair lifted by its henna-ed roots. He at least was happy to see us, and offered to increase our wages to £50 apiece if we started immediately. I managed to get only a couple of pints inside me in the time it took Dod to fix up his drum kit, and Trippy didn't get a chance to drop anything heavy (he's not called Trippy because he falls over his bootlaces) before he was sat in front of a rickety upright piano and swung into 'Ain't Misbehavin''. I let him have three choruses before I got the mouthpiece into my trumpet and took the lead, fluffing the first two bars badly, though nobody seemed to notice.

We'd gone through our repertoire, such as it was when reduced to drums, horn and piano, each taking two solos to cover for the missing trombone, bass, clarinet and banjo, at least twice before we got requests for 'Happy Birthday'. Three or four of them kept the customers quiet – well, actually, anything but quiet – and then the disco's amplifier was fixed by one of the regulars using an ivory-handled nail-file and we had the chance of a breather. I've always said that breathing was a good way to describe

Dod drinking beer; he sort of inhaled it, and I swear I never saw him swallow. I just did my best to keep pace, knowing it would end in tears. Trippy stayed at the bar for two of his favourite Wally Headbanger cocktails (large vodkas with orange and tomato, yes, tomato, juice) then disappeared into the toilet to rifle through his portable medicine chest.

All three of us were pretty much wrecked by midnight and it was just as well that we weren't asked to play again. I don't think Trippy could have actually found the piano, and he was beginning to draw attention to himself by stumbling around the dance floor bumping into clientele – one of whom took him aside and said, 'Darling, how do you get your pupils to shrink so?'

The upshot was, as could have been predicted, that none of us was in a fit state to drive back to London. Veteran cars that run on steam do London to Brighton easily every year. We couldn't. The three of us collapsed in the back of Dod's Bedford van to sleep it off among the mattresses, cardboard boxes and assorted ancient rugs that he keeps there to protect his drum kit when in transit. I woke up first (Rule of Life No 143: when sleeping in a strange place, always wake up first) and liberated two pints of Gold Top from a nearby unguarded milk-float. That was breakfast settled as far as

Dod and I were concerned. Trippy declined, convinced that milk gives you cancer. A quick visit to a seafront Gents and we were on our way back to London before the dawn and commuters, getting to the Gun just after six.

The reason we drove to the Gun was not just a craving for alcohol. It was fairly central for all of us, me for Hackney, Trippy for his squat in Islington and Dod for his council flat in Bethnal Green. Also, I'd left my car parked round the side of the pub facing Bishopsgate. (Rule of Life No 277: always park a car facing away from where you are, to facilitate quick exits.)

Anyway, there we were and there she was.

In the midst of all those Hooray Henries, I naturally assumed she was a bit of a Sloane, though she did not seem to be joining in the general frivolity. The Hooray Henries had actually bought champagne and a couple of bottles of Guinness and were debating among themselves how to mix a Black Velvet. (Two-thirds stout to one-third bubbly, stout goes in first, and the Irish mix it in a jug, not the glass.) She sat slightly apart from them, as though she was not with the party but had just come through the door at the same time, and gave off plenty of God-I'm-bored signals as the Henries fought among themselves to be the first one to pour her a glass. While flicking her blonde-streaked fringe out of her eyes, she managed to clock every other male in the pub, including me, but there was no eye-contact there, nor with anyone else as far as I could tell.

I remember her in detail because of what happened later, of course, but even so, she made quite an impression that morning in the Gun. Some women would have made an impression at that time in the morning if they'd walked in wearing a plastic bin liner; others could have come in their birthday suits and still not got served first. She was neither of them. Pretty, certainly, but not stunning enough to, say, hold up a game of darts.

But she was well dressed, and expensively, and it was the combination that set the heads turning. She had draped a white fur coat so casually over the back of her chair that it couldn't have been worth more than a grand. And although it was a fairly chill October morning outside, and not exactly a greenhouse inside, she was wearing a figure-hugging, strapless dress with long sleeves cut off at the shoulder. In fact, she was dressed in three shades of blue, for the light blue of the dress was offset by navy blue stockings and then high-heeled, really bright electric-blue shoes.

I watched her play with a cigarette for a while and take occasional sips from the

Black Velvet one of the Henries had poured her. They were busy talking among themselves and spilling Guinness down their dinner jackets. They were too far away for me to hear what they were saying, but most people prefer it that way when the Hoorays are around, especially at that time in the morning. Despite a couple of spirited attempts on my part, there was none of the necessary magic eye-contact with her, so I turned back to Trippy and Dod.

Their conversation was par for the course. In other words, Dod was saying nothing, simply puckering his lips alternately around a small snifter of brandy and a cup of hot, sweet coffee, and Trippy was baiting him about Arsenal. You know the patter: 'Are you going to see Arsenal on Saturday or would you prefer live football?' 'Have you heard that Arsenal have lost their Mogadon sponsorship?' So on, so forth.

When it was my turn to buy the next round – bacon sandwiches this time; well, you can drink only so much coffee, can't you? – I stayed at the bar chatting to a bloke I'd once done a few odd jobs for. In the mirror behind the bottles, I saw her get up and leave, trailing, would you believe it, the white fur coat after her.

'Well, that's one way of cleaning the floor,' I said to the barman as he delivered our sarnies.

'Hah, mate, don't fall for that one. She's a sawdust rustler. Soon as she gets outside, she brushes out all our sawdust, sieves it a coupla times, then sells it to the wine bar round on Bishopsgate.'

'Is that a fact?' I asked, all innocent.

'Straight up, mate. How the hell do you think she can afford a coat like that?'

He had a point. A stupid one, and not worth thinking about at that time in the morning. I just delivered the bacon sandwiches.

Dod's disappeared into one of his giant hands. Trippy inspected his one for fried tomato. (He had a thing about tomato skins.) I suddenly felt badly in need of a wash and shave.

'I'm hitting the road, you guys, before the traffic hots up.'

Dod nodded, munching away.

'What's the next gig?' Trippy asked.

'There's a Students' Union do at City University week after next, and I've a couple of pubs lined up wanting some mainline Dixieland for Thanksgiving Day parties next month. Shall I count you in?'

They both nodded, then Trippy asked: 'Nothing this weekend?'

'I'll keep an ear open for you, maybe give you a bell if the phone's still connected in your squat.'

'Of course it is. The guy squatting in the

basement is a GLC councillor; he needs his channels of communication.'

'Okay, I'll see if there's anything doing. See yer around, y'all!'

I wrapped a paper napkin bearing the legend 'Trumans Beers' around my bacon sandwich and munched my way to the door, nodding to a couple of customers I recognized and avoiding the stares of a couple more I probably owed drinks to. As I stepped out on to Brushfield Street, I caught a last glimpse of the Hooray Henries ordering another bottle of what they thought was real champagne before the door swung shut.

It was a dank and overcast morning and still only just light. There were the usual market noises coming from Spitalfields, the crashing of wooden crates, shouted instructions in Cockney dialects that would have defeated Professor Higgins, and deep-throated diesel trucks warming up to ferry sprouts to Sainsbury's and tomatoes to Tesco's. The street itself was littered with the morning's best buys for the wholesalers. Judging from what I trod in, the weekend's bargains were going to be bananas and fresh figs.

I retrieved my trumpet case from the back of Dod's van. We never locked it, as Dod had well over-insured it in the hope of theft. Then I threw the remains of my sandwich to the scavenging pigeons and turned the corner to where I'd parked my taxi.

No, I'm not a cabbie, but I do own a London cab. Second-hand, they're a nice bet if you can get a good one that has been looked after. I had fallen on a little beauty, black bodywork immaculate, as cheap to run, on diesel, as almost anything can be these days in London, highly unlikely to get stolen, never known to get a parking ticket, and an engine that, even with a slightly dubious 180,000 miles on the clock, still ran as sweet as a nut. It has the added advantage that although the Licensed Hackney Carriage plate has been removed and the meter disconnected, certain people simply will not believe it is no longer a proper taxi. Now, I know London pretty well, and I'm an obliging sort of bloke who likes to help people out, and it becomes a real pain trying to stop people like that showing how grateful they are for the lift. How am I supposed to stop them if they want to press money on me?

The girl in the white fur and blue dress was leaning against the left-side doors. It looked as if I had another customer.

'At last,' I heard her breathe. Then she looked me full in the face and said, 'Can you take me up West to Marble Arch? If you're not off duty or anything. I just need to get out of this circus.'

The problem seemed to be that she was lost. I toyed with the idea of showing her around the corner and pointing out Liverpool Street station, which has excellent underground services to the West End (40p a ticket and about 12 minutes if the train turns up). Then I looked her up and down again and thought that if there was anything wrong with her face it might be that her eyes were permanently too big and maybe a fraction too far apart. But sod it, I'm not an optician.

'Marble Arch it is, miss, if you'll bear with me while I get old Armstrong here started.'

'Armstrong?' she asked – they always do – as I let her into the passenger seats. 'As in Louis.'

'That's right, named after my hero.' I was impressed. She couldn't have been more than ten or 11 when Satchmo died.

'I gathered as much from the trumpet.' Observant, too. 'You were in the pub, weren't you.' It was not a question.

Armstrong staggered into life and I let him run for a minute before turning on the heater. As I pulled away, I opened the sliding glass panel so I could talk over my shoulder, and adjusted the driving mirror so I could see her.

'I wouldn't have put you down as a regular at the Gun, miss. They haven't changed the juke-box there since the three-day week.'

'First and last time,' she said, looking out of the window. 'What was the three-day week?'

'Before your time, miss. The miners were on strike and the power stations ran out of coal. The lights kept going out every couple of hours, so the working week was cut to three days. Brilliant. Never had it so good. Going back to five days will be the death of me.'

We were approaching the new Stock Exchange tower, and I narrowly missed a pair of jobbers hurrying to make the first million of the morning. When I looked back in the mirror, she was staring at me.

'Do you have a light?' And she made it sound throaty.

'Sure.' I flipped her a French disposable lighter – I get job-lots of them from a Channel Ferry stewardess I know.

'Then you'll probably have a cigarette as well.'

I laughed and tossed a packet of Gold Flake over my shoulder.

'What on earth are these? My God, they don't have filters!'

'I don't smoke much, but when I do, I like a cigarette to be ... well ... satisfying. They're an old and distinguished brand. Been around for years.'

She closed the packet without taking one and held it and the lighter over my shoulder, then dropped both in my lap. I wondered if it was her way of letting me see that she had no rings on her left hand.

'You're a very curious cabby, you know.'

'Oh yeah? And why's that, then?' In the mirror, I saw her bend forward to pull down the rumble seat behind me to put her feet on.

'To start with, you drink coffee and cognac at seven in the morning in the company of people who don't seem to wash their clothes all that often. Then you tell me that your cab is called Armstrong and you come on like the old man of the hills about three-day weeks and cigarettes that could have come off a troopship going to Gallipoli. Yet the weirdest thing of all is that you never started your meter running.'

They often notice that there is something wrong with the meter as viewed from the back seat, but they are never quite sure what. From the street it simply looks as if the cab is off duty, but inside I have had a neat little conversion job done incorporating one of the latest fell-off-the-back-of-a-lorry tape-decks wired to an amplifier on the dashboard. Well, why not? It's a great conversation-starter.

As I slowed to allow some pedestrians across the zebra crossing near St Paul's, I selected a tape and slotted it in. With a bit of practice, it can be the same movement as a cabby setting his meter running. I flicked on the rear speakers and adjusted the volume to about half strength.

'It's Dire Straits,' she squealed delightedly, moving into the middle seat. 'Is it the "Alchemy" concert?'

'No. I've got that if you'd prefer it, but this is their concert at Wembley this summer.'

'I didn't know they'd made an album of it.'

'They didn't. This is bootlegged.'

'How exciting.' She didn't look excited; she was just as cool as she had been in the Gun.

'It was a great concert,' I said, to keep the conversation flowing at this stunningly high intellectual level. 'Well, they all were, 'cos they were there for about three weeks. I thought everybody in London had been. Princess Diana went.'

'Yeah, well, she did ask me to make up a foursome but I was washing my hair that night.' Sarky, too.

'I know it couldn't possibly compare to the Gun and your swinging breakfast scene. What were you up to? Discoing all the way from cocoa to cornflakes?'

'Christ!' She breathed it more than said it. 'You only saw them for two minutes and you realised they were a bunch of wallies. I'd been with them since midnight and I didn't twig until about half past one.'

'So why stay with them?'

'Because I don't get out much these days. And–' she stared into the mirror – 'because I don't have any money on me. Not a penny.

21

So it's a good job you're not a real cab, isn't it?'

One of the really big pluses about running a taxi, or what looks like one, is that you can swan up and down Oxford Street without getting nicked now that civilian traffic has been banned, though of course you still get the odd Swede or Dutchman who gets lost and wonders why all the buses and black cabs and I are hooting horns at him.

We had a good run straight through from Tottenham Court, and even the lights were with us. As we approached the Arch, I could see the Toff outside the tube station entrance selling newspapers and insulting tourists, so all seemed right with the world. They say that tourism will be Britain's biggest industry by the year 2000. Well, every industry has its Luddites, and the Toff is a one-man protest movement dedicated to humiliating visitors, fiddling their change and misdirecting the unwary. I thought about giving him a hoot but decided against it.

'Here we are, madam,' I said over my shoulder. 'Where can I drop you?'

'Do you know Seymour Place? Round the corner.'

'Sure. Been swimming there.'

'Swimming?'

'In the pools down the Sports Centre.'

'You mean there's a health club down here?'

22

'Not the sort of club you're probably used to, darlin'; it's the local council pool – you know, GLC Working For London – but it's got a sauna and fings.'

'And it's full of fake Cockneys like you, huh? Spare me the cheap imitations and just take a right, then a left. Okay?'

'Soiternlay, ma'am,' I said in bad bog Irish. 'De customer is always roight.'

She said nothing, but in the mirror I could see her lip gloss part ever so slightly, which is what passes for a smile these days among the supercool. On the tape, Dire Straits swung into 'Walk of Life'. ('You're not supposed to stand on the seats,' Mark Knopfler had told about 7,000 people every night for three weeks, 'but if you all do it, who's gonna stop you?') I felt dirty, but it was the clothes-slept-in sort of grime that could be easily removed with a shower. Otherwise, pretty good.

'Stop here. On the left. Park behind the Mini.'

I did as instructed and wondered if I should get out and open the door for her. She beat me to it, and I thought: well, that's that. Then she said: 'You'll have to come in for your fare. I told you I don't have any cash on me.'

American Express would have done nicely. But I didn't say it.

Her block of apartments was called Sedgeley House. It was one of those custom-built blocks of about a dozen flats that look like left-over sets from 1930s sci-fi movies and are made of grey stone that turns streaky brown when it rains. The double-lock front door opened into a small entrance hall that had a bank of pigeonholes for mail and a desk with an elderly night-watchman (probably called a porter) pouring milk from a freshly opened pint into a Snoopy mug of tea.

'Oh ... er ... morning ... er...'

She gave the old boy a regal wave and stepped smartly into the open lift before he had time to address her by name. There had been no names on the mailboxes either; not that it would have helped, as I didn't know which flat. Yet.

It turned out to be No 11, on the top floor, and it was decorated like a Laura Ashley showroom.

'Nice pad,' I said, watching her drop her bunch of keys on a coffee table and then the fur coat over the back of the chair.

'Bit twee, don't you think?'

'Each to her own,' I said to the back of her neck as she continued across the room and through another door without pausing.

'Back in a minute. Put the radio on.' She didn't turn round.

There, on top of a stripped-pine chest of drawers, was a large, chrome ghetto-blaster that anyone with a degree in electrical engineering could work easily. After a bit of fumbling, I tuned into Radio 4, which had bad news for commuters on Southern Region and a weather report depressing enough to induce mass suicide north of Watford.

I had just time to take in the video-recorder and, through the connecting door, the microwave and jug-style kettle (all portable and saleable) in the kitchen when I heard her behind me.

'Well, then. We'd better settle your fare, hadn't we?'

She was posing in the doorway of the bedroom; and I mean posing, hands on hips, head angled back and one leg crooked slightly in front of the other. She still wore the high-heeled, really electric-blue shoes and the navy blue stockings, which were the sort that stayed up by themselves and didn't need a suspender belt. I'd seen them before in the sort of magazine that Dod bought for the dirty pictures and I borrowed to read the book reviews. That was all she was wearing.

The BBC timepips cracked out of the radio to announce that it was 8.00 am. And time for the news. It was going to be one of those days.

CHAPTER TWO

It was in the Mimosa Club that I next saw her, about five months later. Okay, so I'd forgotten to write. Or phone. Nobody's perfect.

I was playing about half a dozen frilly but pretty repetitive riffs along with an alto-sax man called Bunny, who was just as bored as I was. We were backing a teenage trio called Peking, who were into electrified Afro-Asian rock, whatever that was, and who were destined to go far. They had a girl lead singer who also played the electric plastic lids that pass for a drum kit nowadays. She was good, if incomprehensible, and quite a looker, despite the salmon-pink Mohican haircut. The other two Pekingetts played keyboards, didn't look old enough to get served in a pub and were probably designing clothes by computer in their spare time.

One of them at least could write music and had scored out a few bars to give us a theme, but we were under strict instructions to stick to the breaks and not to improvise. Which was a pity, because Bunny was very good and could have done a lot for their arrangements, given half a chance. But then

Bunny was really interested in only one thing, sex, and was halfway to making the girl drummer before the end of the first set.

It was a way of life with Bunny, who always went for quantity rather than quality and, where possible, married women. It all stemmed from finding his wife in bed with a bloke from the office. Well, not so much that as finding out during the ritual punch-up that always follows such discoveries that the affair had been going on for three years and two months, the marriage being three years and three months old. Once the divorce had been finalised, the flat in Muswell Hill sold off and the goldfish divided between them, Bunny had packed in his job as an insurance broker and taken to the streets with his alto. He was good with it and earned a regular wage as a theatre-pit musician and a session man on the odd recording. On warm summer evenings, he polished up an ancient soprano sax (making a comeback after Sting's 'Dream of the Blue Turtles' album) and busked in Covent Garden outside the Punch and Judy. I told you he was good; you have to pass an audition to busk there these days. But it was all only a means to financing his hobby of women.

Not that he needed the cash to wine and dine them or buy them expensive presents. Bunny needed loot to finance his campaign, and it was at times as spontaneous and lighthearted as a U-Boat trailing a convoy. I mean, Bunny thought in terms of this woman being worth x gallons of petrol and that woman was $y+1$ pints of beer. It was very cold-hearted ... I mean, not the sort of thing I could do. Bunny always knew the best days for shopping at Sainsbury's (usually the day women picked up the family allowance) and when every ladies darts team in the area was playing away (home matches sometimes attracted husbands). And the worst thing about it was, he was successful. And with chat-up lines like: 'Hello, I'm Bunny. I suppose a fuck's out of the question?' I ask you! I once suggested a more subtle approach, such as a sock filled with sand, and I do believe he considered it for a day or two.

So it was not surprising that Bunny saw her first. In between numbers, he nudged me in the ribs and whispered, 'Third table back near the bar.'

Between the strobes that lit up Peking, I could make out the two girls at the table now in the crosshairs of Bunny's randy sights. If the Mimosa had been smoke-filled and dimly lit, it could have been a scene from a 1940s movie scripted by Chandler. But the Mimosa could never be smoke-filled as it was far too draughty, and the only dimly-lit parts were where the odd light-bulb had blown. The one on the right,

wearing what appeared to be a pink jumpsuit, was a stranger to me, but the other was
Jo, the girl from the Gun and Seymour
Place. Well, at least I'd remembered her
name.

'I think you could be in there, boy. I know
the one on the left.'

Bunny perked up at that and put a real zip
into the intro to the last number of the set,
a good standard rocker that, with a stronger
bass line, would stand a chance in the
charts. We both enjoyed ourselves with it to
the extent that neither of us noticed the two
women had left.

The Peking trio didn't bother with a bow
– in fact the audience didn't even rate two
fingers – they just slumped offstage leaving
Bunny and me to pack up our reeds, mouth-
pieces, mutes and instruments, as the disco
at the other end of the club came alive. In
the one room backstage, which doubled as a
storeroom, dressing-room and bar cellar,
the girl drummer was dabbing something
on to a lace handkerchief held near her
nose. One of the keyboard players was half-
way down a fat joint. He inhaled and held it
out to me. I took a draw and tried to see
what the girl was popping.

'Do you want some snap?' she asked
between sniffs.

I shook my head as I exhaled. 'No, thanks.
Isobutyl nitrite really screws you up. Didn't

29

you know?'

'And smoking is very old-fashioned,' she said, inhaling deeply.

'So's sex,' I pointed out. She turned her back on me and sat down on an empty beer keg. I handed the joint back to the keyboard player, who was crumbling a couple of white tablets into an open can of Carlsberg Special Brew. These kids were determined not to get to middle age – say 21 or 22.

The third member of Peking came out of the communal toilet, zipping up his flies. He at least seemed to be bent on staying straight, but then again, he was their business manager as well.

'I'll take the T-shirts, lads,' he nosed in a Scouser accent.

I had almost forgotten that we'd had to be in costume for the performance. Well, actually it was only the T-shirt worn long over our Levi's, but they were specially printed for the group with a reproduction of the poster from the epic *55 Days at Peking*. You know, the one with Charlton Heston and David Niven and Robert Helpmann and Leo Genn playing Chinese generals. It's bound to come up in Trivial Pursuit one of these days.

I peeled mine off and Bunny did the same, pausing only to flex his pectorals (at least I think they were his pectorals) at the drum-meress. She ignored him and emptied more stuff onto her handkerchief. The plastic bottle she was using was a commercial brand American 'popper' labelled 'Liquid Incense'. A likely story.

'Mr Stubbly's got your dough,' said the guy collecting the T-shirts.

From my trumpet case I took a rather crumpled shirt and began to put it on, along with a wide, black-felt, kipper-style tie that was 12 years out of fashion but was useful for funerals and wiping dust off records and anyway was the only one I had. Bunny had balanced his overnight bag (he never went anywhere without it) on a stack of beer crates and was sorting out his battery razor, deodorant, aftershave, clean shirt, fake-half-sovereign medallion on a chain and so on. I was getting changed because Stubbly, the club owner, had strict smartness rules for club patrons, even if they were virtually full-time employees like me. Bunny was getting tarted up because it was crumpet-hunting time.

'Everything go okay?' I asked the man from Peking, who was carefully folding up our T-shirts and putting them back into plastic bags.

'Fine. The set went fine, man, but to no avail.' He took the joint out of his fellow bandsman's mouth and drew deep. 'Good sounds, but the Man ran.'

'Who did?' I asked.

31

'Who did what?' asked Bunny.

'*The* Man – from Waxworks Records. He was here to lend us an ear with a view to a contract.'

'Yeah,' said Bunny, squirting aerosol into his arm-pits, 'I saw Lloyd earlier on.'

That's him,' said the young Pekinger. 'Lloyd Allen. These cruds didn't believe he'd come.'

The girl drummer made a face at him, then buried it back in her handkerchief.

'Is Lloyd talent-scouting for Waxworks now? What happened to his string of female wrestlers?' I asked because I was genuinely interested, but the lad from Peking seemed surprised.

'Oh, he's still running them,' said Bunny casually. 'That's why he popped next door. Four of his girls are doing a tag match in mud tonight at the Eldorado. First show's at 10.30. I should think he'll be back after that.'

'Mud-wrestling? He's gone to watch some tarts fighting. In mud?'

The aspiring megastar was rapidly slipping down dissolution hill, but Bunny took pity on him.

'We can pop round there ourselves, if you like. I'm a member.' He would be. 'I'll take er ... er...'

'The name's Geoff, with a G,' said the only member of Peking not out of his skull.

'All right, Geoff, if Angel here agrees to pick up my wages from Mr Stubbly, we can go off now and catch the show at the Eldorado.'

Bunny looked at me and I nodded an okay.

'That's it then, let's roll – and let's be careful in there.' He did his *Hill Street Blues* routine. 'Keep those two at the bar going, I'll be back.'

He walked out, alto case under one arm and Geoff under the other. He didn't come back, of course. It was two days later that I found him to pass on his wages. He was in a launderette washing mud off his shirt.

And by the time I'd got to the bar, they weren't there. Ken the barman and I did the full routine.

'Did you see what happened to the two birds who were at Table Five when the band was on?' I asked, after ordering a Pils.

'You mean the rather svelte one in the frilly blue number and her butch mate with the skinhead cut and the pink jumpsuit?'

'Yeah, that's them.' I gritted my teeth, knowing what was coming.

'Nobody like that in here tonight, mate.' He went back to polishing glasses.

'Oh, come on, Ken, at least get a new scriptwriter. What happened to them?'

'They left. During the last number. What more can I say?'

At this rate, Ken's conversation was going to keep me at the bar about as long as the glass of Pils. I considered returning to the dressing-room to see what the girl drummer was doing, but decided against it. Head cases like that I could live without. I surveyed the disco floor. Nothing there; well, nothing spare anyway. So it looked like an early night.

But first, there was the problem of getting our wages out of Bill Stubbly. In itself, a diplomatic mission no more difficult than, say, Munich if it was 1938 and you were Czech.

Bill Stubbly, the proud owner of the Mimosa Club, was a bluff, no-nonsense Yorkshireman who had no business to be in showbusiness. Well, not in Soho, anyway. Despite all his drawbacks – his basic honesty, his total lack of entrepreneurial flair, his status as a happily-married, middle-aged man with two kids – he survived. There were rules, of course, by which he survived; some of his own making, many not. He loathed the drugs trade in any shape or form (thank God he never went into his dressing-room), partly because drugs to a Yorkshireman meant aspirin and partly because it would push him straight into the claws of the gangs and dealers. Yet there he was on Dean Street with a firetrap of a club well inside Triad territory, and you're telling me he wasn't paying somebody somewhere? He got into the club business after coming to London for the first time to a Rugby League Final in the '60s. It was as simple as that. He and his mates had a weekend on the pop in the big city, and Bill never did turn up for the Monday morning shift down't t'pit. The Mimosa's main attraction was its drinking hours. Basically, it opened when the pubs were shut in the afternoon, providing a useful social service for the army of thirsty lost souls searching for a drink in the desert hours of 3.00 to 5.30. Interestingly enough, the only identifiable ethnic minority group to be actively banned from entering the Mimosa were Rugby League supporters down in London for the Cup. How's that for class betrayal?

I found Bill standing where the hat-check girl would have been if the Mimosa had run to a full-time hat-check girl.

In most Soho clubs, the cloakroom receptionist person, as we have to say these days, usually doubles as the fill-in stripper. The fill-in, that is, between the bands, other strippers, comedians (rare), strippers, comediennes (a breed rapidly multiplying), more strippers, live sex acts and guest strippers. They can, of course, be male or female, depending on the club, the street it's in, the time of day, and the workload of the local Vice Squad.

The Mimosa being Bill's club and Dean Street being healthily hetero this year meant that it just had to be different. There were no strippers of any kind at the Mimosa anymore, and Bill Stubbly even resisted the white heat of modern technology by not showing blue movies. Pimps and tarts were discouraged unless they were off duty and bona-fide customers. No pick-ups were allowed and no bills were ever loaded when a trio of 'hostesses' turned up at the unsuspecting businessman's table to drink Malvern water from a champagne bottle at 30 quid a go. It was amazing that Bill made any money at all.

'Well, guess who's a popular feller today, then.' Bill's opening line was not a question. It never was. I would probably have said no out of sheer shock if he'd actually asked me if I'd come for my money.

'I know it went okay, Bill,' I beamed, 'but nobody's asked me for an autograph yet. They're not a bad band, you know. Got 'em signed up yet?' That was a bitchy crack, but Bill's ambitions to turn the Mimosa into a Cavern Club and discover his own version of the Beatles were a standing joke. Bill wouldn't recognise star quality if it bit him in the leg.

'You reckon they're a bit tasty, then?' He looked up from under his eyebrows at me while he ran his tongue along the gummed strip of a roll-your-own.

'Could go far, I think, given a new writer

36

or a pro arranger. The girl's got a good voice and the two guys have plenty of good ideas. You might have a winner there, Billy, if you play your cards right.'

'Too late, old lad,' sighed Bill through a cloud of Old Holborn. 'That smarmy spade Lloyd Allen has snapped them up with a bit of flim-flam about a recording contract.'

I put a friendly hand on the shoulder of his shiny dinner jacket. 'I know they're all black when they come up from the pit in York-shire, Billy, but you're not supposed to call them spades down here in the big city.'

'Where I come from, lad, we call a spade a fookin' shovel. And we'd call you a young tyke with a loose lip. It never does to be too lippy before you've been paid, young Angel.' He smiled enough to show how much all that soft Pennine water had stained his teeth. (It couldn't have been the 50 roll-ups a day.) 'That's an 'elluva name you've got, you know. Fit...'

'Okay, okay, I've read my passport. Now, about my wages...'

'And Bunny's. Don't forget the sax player. He's good, that one. Real talent.'

'Thanks, Bill, you're all tact.'

'How come he's got such a funny name as well? Bunny. Where did he get a name like Bunny?'

'He likes lettuce. How about some cash so he can buy some more?'

Taking a deep breath, Stubbly reached into his back pocket and produced a wad of notes thick enough to make him walk with a limp. Licking a forefinger and thumb, he peeled off two tenners.

'I'll take Bunny's as well. He's gone boozing.' Well, it was worth a try.

'That is Bunny's as well,' said Bill, dead serious. 'The sodding band only got 60. Said they would bring their fan club, but I never noticed them. Didn't even get one of the usual scroungers from *Time Out* or *Rolling Stone*. Not even one of those freebies you get thrown at you at the tube station.'

'Now, I might be able to help you there, Bill me old mate.' I slipped the two thin notes into my back pocket and tried to imagine how much a wad like Bill's would spoil the cut of my stonewasheds. 'I know a bird who works on *Mid-Week* magazine–' I didn't tell Bill that she was one of the girls at the tube station giving copies away – 'and she can get a review in for me. They've published some stuff of mine before.'

Bill reached for his back pocket again but then thought better of it.

'Well, you do what you can, lad, and there'll be a drink in it for you. Oh, and another thing, there's a bird looking for you.'

The evening suddenly seemed brighter.

'What, the one who was on Table Five earlier on?'

'Now don't be previous, lad.' When Bill started using Yorkshire homilies like that, it usually meant he had something bad to tell you. 'She turned up this morning, name of Mrs Bateman. Very interested in you, she was. In fact, she was very interested in all of us at the Mimosa.'

'I'm getting a very nervous feeling about this, Bill. Who was she, Bill?'

'She's a National Insurance Inspector, old son. You haven't been paying your stamps, have you?'

'Oh, shit.'

I got back to Hackney well before midnight, having picked up a Chinkie takeaway en route. As I let myself into the house, I marvelled at how hot the food stayed in those metal containers, particularly the oyster sauce from the fried beef that was dripping down my leg.

I was balancing the takeaway, my trumpet case and the door keys when Fenella appeared on the first landing. I bit my tongue and resisted the temptation to ask why she was dressed as a schoolgirl. It probably was her own old school uniform, though the white nylon shirt bulged in places it never had when she was in the hockey team.

'Hi there, Fenella,' I said. You always have to be the first to speak with Fenella. 'How's Lisabeth?'

'She's in a swoon,' Fenella said sweetly, though not without, I thought, a slight touch of malice. 'It was your cat. He's brought in a rat again, and Lisabeth was in the loo when he climbed through the window.'

I started up the stairs towards my flat on the floor above hers. 'Did you say in the loo or on it?'

Fenella put a hand to her mouth to stifle a giggle, but she was brought up short by a stentorian bellow from inside her flat.

'Binky!' (Fenella's surname was, sadly, Binkworthy.) 'Are you talking to a man?'

'Only Mr Angel.' Only!

'Get yourself in here this instant!'

Fenella mouthed, 'See you,' and disappeared in a flurry of pleated grey skirt, and I continued up the next flight. I think she fancies me; have thought so for a while. Then I thought about a Lisabeth crazed with jealousy and decided that voluntary castration might be the least painful option.

I did my juggling act again to get my flat door open, and in trying to thump the light switch, I felt the top come off the crab and sweetcorn soup.

Springsteen had come in via the cat flap in the flat door, a little structural alteration that our landlord hadn't noticed yet, thank Allah. He was sitting in the middle of the floor in the 'cello position,' one back leg straight up in the air, washing some mysterious part of his anatomy.

He had left his kill, a bundle of half-chewed white fur, in the entrance to the bedroom. I had news for Fenella and Lisabeth. It wasn't a rat, and Springsteen had found yet another way into Mr Cohen's pet shop around the corner.

Some evenings are never dull.

CHAPTER THREE

The communal phone for the house is nailed to the wall near the front door. Our landlord, the gentle and generous Mr Nassim (well, have you tried getting a place in Hackney lately?), had thoughtfully installed extension bells on each landing, which meant that the phone woke me and everybody else the next morning just after six.

Well, almost everybody. It would take more than a phone, unless you applied it physically, to get Lisabeth out of her pit before noon. But from the flat above mine, Frank Asmoyah appeared, wearing the bottom half of a Nike jogging suit in a tasteful light tan colour to set off his ebony skin all the better, and below me, Fenella opened her door cautiously, displaying only the top half of what appeared to be pink Snoopy pyjamas.

I had remembered to wrap a towel round my midriff and was quite prepared to save Fenella's blushes and answer the damn thing before Frank showed me up by jogging downstairs without breaking sweat. But it was the quietly strange Mr Goodson from the ground-floor flat who got there first.

Of all the weird people living in our house,

Mr Goodson was undoubtedly the flakiest. I mean, he didn't smoke, drink, go out, play loud music, indulge in unusual sexual activities or take drugs, and he could do the *Guardian* crossword. Mr Goodson never invited anyone into his flat and never went to parties in the others. He left the house every morning at 8.15 am. And returned at 5.55 pm. No-one saw him at week-ends. He was something in local Government, but not much. He stood there in a threadbare, checked dressing-gown, which came almost all the way down to some old-fashioned leather slippers, and held out the receiver as if it had Aids.

'It's for you,' he said, dead straight, as if he'd never seen a British Telecom advert. He probably hadn't.

I padded downstairs clutching my towel on my hips, but Fenella had retreated back into Lisabeth's lair before I could think up a smart remark. Mr Goodson was holding the phone at arm's length and moving gently from one foot to the other as if he was barefoot on cold lino.

I tried a disarming smile on Mr Goodson, although at that time of the morning it was no more than quarter volume, as I took the phone from him.

'Sorry about this, Mr G. It's probably my American friend Ray. He always forgets about the time difference.'

I actually do have an American friend called Ray who does forget the time difference, especially when he's stoned, but Mr Goodson didn't look as if he believed me. He just shuffled off back to his flat, opening and closing the door the barest minimum so that I could see nothing of his inner sanctum. I really will have to go and borrow a cup of sugar one of these days.

'Hello?'

'Is that you, Angel?' The voice was female, so unless he was on something spectacular, it wasn't Ray.

'Who wants him?'

'It's me. Jo. I saw you in the Mimosa last night. We met last year.'

'Oh yeah. Hi. Were you in the club?' Mr Cool. 'I don't... Do you know what time it is?'

'Yes, and I'm sorry but ... there are reasons. I must see you to ... to ask you something.'

'Ask away.' I was curious, and also worried that I couldn't remember her last name.

'Not now, it's too difficult. Can you meet at Champnas on Duke Street this afternoon at three?'

'I suppose so if...'

'Thanks. I mean it. Thanks.' She hung up.

I went back to bed. What could it be she wanted to see me about? After a five-month gap it could hardly be physical passion.

Maybe she wanted to tell me how much she'd enjoyed my backing Peking at the Mimosa. Maybe she'd discovered something missing from her flat after I'd left that morning, and my appearance at the club had reminded her. It could be anything. Life's like that; bloody worrying. Still, if it had been anything bad – surely to God she wasn't pregnant; not these days – she would have come round to play out the big scene. But then I never give out my address after just one date. (Rule of Life No 23.)

Come to think of it, I never give out my phone number either.

It seemed like only a couple of minutes later that Frank woke me to remind me that I was doing a job for him, but in fact it was after 9.00 am. Frank knocked once, came in and selected a Zappa tape from the collection near the stereo and started it at full volume, then left. You can tell Frank's woken me up before.

I was reaching across the bed to turn the volume down to a dull roar when Salome, Frank's wife, came in with a mug of coffee. This was always Phase Two of Frank's plan, and the bit I looked forward to most.

Salome was wearing a white shirt and black tie and a red-leather trouser suit with the trousers tucked into short, red-leather boots.

'Just what does it take to get you up, Fitz-roy?' She busied herself clearing old copies of *Melody Maker*, paperbacks and empty Chinese takeaway containers from the drop-leaf table that formed approximately one-third of my furniture.

'If you hadn't called me that, and if Frank wasn't so much bigger than me, I'd invite you in here and answer that.' I patted the duvet, which had apparently attempted to strangle my legs during the night.

Salome smiled back ravishingly and put on a puzzled expression. She held her right forefinger, long and red-nailed, to her chin.

'You know, Angel,' she said huskily, 'I think you have something there.'

'Really?' I wished that I'd brushed my teeth.

'Mmmm. Yes, you're right.'

'I am?'

'Yeah. Frank is so much bigger...'

She squealed with laughter as I threw a pillow at her; she caught it and flung it back hard, and then was out of the door and clacking her heels up the stairs.

Frank and Salome Asmoyah were what I called Black Anglo Saxon Upwardly Mobiles. BASUMs – though I never said this to Salome when Frank was around. He was a trainee legal beagle in Holborn, one of those who don't have enough cash to buy a round of drinks for three years and then one day they're phoning you from their customised Porsche. Salome was the big earner of the partnership. She was an analyst in a City stockbroking firm specialising in the leisure market, which meant free holidays put down as vital research and the possibility of a six-figure 'golden hello' should she be good enough to be poached by a rival firm. Still, she worked hard for it, starting at 8.00 every morning and having lunch every day at La Bastille or Le Gamin.

They had taken the day off together in order to work on their new flat in Limehouse, for which they were mortgaged up to the hilt as they had found it only after Limehouse became trendy. I had been hired to act as transport for an industrial floor sander that Frank had rented for the day before realizing that it wouldn't fit in the back of their VW Golf.

Frank also needed a hand carting the damn thing up four flights of stairs, partly because it was heavy and partly because Salome couldn't risk getting oil on her leather suit. She was there not to do any sanding, but to make cups of tea and consult very expensive books on interior design by people with names like Jocasta. The renovation of their flat was to be a shared experience, they said, and so far they had been sharing it for six months. The mortgage, you see, was so much that they could only afford to do things piecemeal. At the moment, the bathroom was the only room worth visiting, but today we were converting the largest empty room into a lounge smart enough for Salome to have the sort of dinner-party she wouldn't invite me to.

I plugged in the sander and showed Frank how to work it. Being multi-talented, intelligent, good at sport and physically attractive to women, he was, of course, totally useless when it came to anything practical. His main achievement of the morning had been to fasten the shoulder-straps on his Levi overalls. When I left him there, just after noon, he had his Sony Walkman on and was waltzing the sander around in a cloud of sawdust. I suppose I should have told him about the bag that goes on the end to collect the dust, but no doubt Salome would. She was experimenting on a bedroom wall with spray paints and stencils of exotic birds when I told her I was off and would be back by 5.00 to return the sander.

'Now remember, my Angel,' she said, 'if you can't be careful, at least be good.'

'You, Salome, darling, are a female chauvinist sow,' I said, running for the door before she could turn the spray paint on me.

I got back to our little Hackney home from home just in time to meet our esteemed landlord, Mr Nassim Nassim, coming out after one of his monthly tours of inspection.

We called him that because when we first tried to ascertain his surname, he said it was too difficult for us and just stick to Nassim. So we did. As landlords go – and let's face it, who likes paying rent? – Nassim was an absolute diamond. As long as the rent came through on time and we residents didn't actually blow the house up (unlike the last place I lived down in Southwark), then he left us alone. Once a month he came to re-count the walls and check that nobody had ringed the electricity meter. As a devout Muslim, he always got somebody who wasn't to buy the crate of Scotch he always smuggled back to Pakistan on his annual holiday there to look up his family. At £40 a bottle on the black market there, it almost paid for his bucket-shop ticket, and as I had undertaken to perform the distasteful act of buying the stuff for him that year, I was his blue-eyed boy. Mind you, if he asks me again, I'll make sure I get a bigger discount from Stan round at the off-licence.

Nassim was, however, a chatterer, and for someone who had been speaking English for less than half his life, he couldn't half rabbit. So I jogged up the steps with a smile and a loud 'Good morning,' and no intention of stopping to pass the time of day.

'Ah... Good morning, Flat Three,' he beamed, making it sound like I was one of the Hampshire 'Flat-Threes'. 'I have news for you.'

That sort of slowed me down as I eased past him through the doorway, but I knew better than to stop.

'I can explain about the door, Mr Nassim,' I offered cheerfully.

'No, no, dear boy...' By this time, he was talking to the back of my head as I reached the stairs. '...You had a visitor while I was here.'

'Oh well, never mind. Life's like that. Sometimes you're in when people call, sometimes you're in Limehouse. We're all playthings of the gods...'

I was half-way up the stairs when he said: 'It was an exceedingly charming young woman.'

Now call me a sucker – many do – but I stopped and turned. 'Wouldn't have been my sister, would it?' I said.

'No, no,' smiled Nassim, brushing an imaginary fleck of dust from his Burberry. 'A professional lady. A married lady. A Mrs Boatman or something similar. I think she wanted to sell you some insurance. She said she was from the National, or similar.'

I started upstairs again. 'Thanks, Mr Nassim, but you know we don't encourage door-to-door sales-persons, whatever their sex.'

I made it to my door and had the key turned before he remembered to shout, 'What you mean, you can explain about the door?'

50

'Champnas,' I discovered later, was Hindi for 'squeeze,' and one of the root words of 'shampoo.' Now there's not, as they say in the best circles, many people who know that. Come to think of it, there's not many people who would give a toss one way or the other about it.

The patrons did, though. Oh yes, Champnas was an 'in' place. So in, you got a choice of decaffeinated coffee even if you weren't having a haircut. In fact, having a haircut seemed to be just a rather tedious consequence of enjoying the experience of being there. It was a unisex salon (do they still call them that?) with the requisite number of nubile 16-year-old Youth Opportunity girls called Sharon or Cheryl (they'll be Dianas and Sarahs soon) to wash your hair and massage your scalp before the bossy ones called Shirley or Jeanette turned up to snip away for half an hour and charge you 20 quid. Looking around at the Sharons and Cheryls, I was glad Bunny was elsewhere, as I was having trouble controlling myself, but I made a mental note to bring him here one afternoon as a treat.

I said I was waiting for someone, and they accepted that, so I settled down to flip through *Motor-Cycle News* – it was either that or *Good Housekeeping* – thinking I was early. Then a body emerged from a chair that could have doubled in a dentist's surgery and a pair of jeans you'd have thought were sprayed on moved towards me.

'Hello, Jo,' I said, recognising the electric-blue shoes, though nothing else seemed the same. She'd been cropped somewhere between a Grace Jones and an Annie Lennox, circa 1984 – short, square and spiky – and her make-up flared red up her cheekbones. Apart from the jeans, she was wearing a batwing-sleeved grey shirt and no bra. And it wasn't even Easter.

'Thanks for coming,' she said, and I bit my tongue.

She paid her bill and asked if we could have two more coffees, which sent one of the Cheryls scurrying off, and sat down beside me. I watched closely to see if the jeans split, but somehow they didn't. Whatever she had to say, she was going to say in the foyer of her hairdresser's. I felt relaxed. It wouldn't be that crucial. I couldn't be that wrong.

We kissed. Just briefly. I appreciated the fact that her lipstick probably wasn't dry, and I got the impression that it wouldn't be dry for a while yet. But then, her knee came to rest near mine and she didn't move it. Sometimes I rate knee-contact as a surer sign than anything else.

'You didn't keep in touch,' she said, but it was non-accusatory.

'And you never wrote but then I never expected your sort would you just take what you can and disappear into the night I know your sort...' There was more, but you get the flavour. Attack is the best form of etc.

She laughed and it was a good laugh and could have been the first one she'd had for a time.

'You're worse than I was told,' she smiled, 'and yes, I'll have one of your horrid cigarettes if you've got one.'

I dug into the pocket of my leather jacket for them. It was a friendly old jacket that I'd had since university, and though they said that distressed leather was okay to be seen in, this was so distressed it was paranoid.

We lit up. She looked around and saw nobody was in hearing distance, but just to make sure, she waited until the duty Cheryl had brought us some coffee, which she paid for with a fiver.

Then she said, 'I'm in trouble.'

'Well, blow me,' I said. 'No, on second thoughts, tell me about it.' And at least it raised a smile. 'But we can go somewhere else if you prefer it.'

'No, it's got to be here and now. I might not get ... away again.'

She drew on the cigarette and then she watched the smoke as she exhaled. For what seemed like an awful long time, she said nothing. It got to the stage where perhaps she wasn't going to say anything, so that part of me that is really a knight in tinfoil armour blew it all by jumping up and speaking out.

'Look, Jo, we're not old friends. We're not even good friends, but there was something between us for a brief moment, and in my book that means at the very least that we should listen to each other if we have a problem. You have a problem and you want to tell me. I don't know why me and I don't really care. If I can help, I will. If I can't, I'll tell you. Can I say fairer than that?'

Another one of the young Cheryls appeared with a saucer full of coins from behind a potted plant big enough to hold a squad of Japanese who didn't know the war was over.

'Your change, madam,' she said as she'd been rehearsed, and waited, poised.

Jo looked up at her and smiled. As she did so, I noticed how cleverly her hairdresser had flecked silver highlights in among the mousey blonde roots. She waved the change away as if blessing a church offerings plate, then turned back to me.

'That was a nice speech and probably more than you've ever said to me before put together. It makes it more difficult for me, but I need to ask a favour.'

(Rule of Life No 477: when a woman admits it's difficult to ask for something,

54

leave immediately.)

'Go ahead, it costs nothing to ask.' Why don't I listen to myself?

'I've had something stolen and I need it back and quickly.'

'Do you know who?'

'Yes, but I don't know where she is. Well, not now.'

'She?'

'Carol. Carol Flaxman. She was a friend of mine.'

'Until when?'

'Last night.'

'She's the one you were with at the club?'

'Yes,' she said quietly, giving me an up-from-under innocent surprise look that didn't quite work now she'd had her fringe chopped. 'Did you see her?'

'Only from the stage. You'd both gone by the time I came looking for you.'

She glanced down into her coffee. 'I'm flattered you looked.'

'I'm flattered you came to see me play.' I gave her a flash of my standard charm smile but pulled the plug on it when she said, with appalling honesty:

'Oh, we didn't come to see you. I didn't even know you'd be there. We came to see the band–'

'Peking.'

'Yeah, Peking. It was Carol's idea, because she knows the girl who plays the drums.

That's why I thought you could help, if you knew her too.'

I decided to join her in a cigarette, though these days I tried to hold back until night-fall.

'I don't follow. You think this Carol has gone to the drummer's pad?' She nodded. 'Then I don't see the problem. I can get you a phone number at least, if not an address. We can go round there and see her...'

'No, I don't want to see her again. Ever. That's what I want you to do. I'll pay you if you help me.'

'Help you do what, exactly? No, wait.' She was about to speak, but I reached out and touched her knee, and felt her flinch. 'Just who is this Carol person and what has she stolen?'

Jo took a deep breath and exhaled slowly the way people are taught to by psychia-trists. It's not a bad way to ease the whirling pits in the stomach when the stress takes over. Neat gin's good too.

'I met Carol at university four – no, five – years ago. She was heavily into women's politics; still is. She drops in and out, taking a year off from her course, then going back and then going abroad for a year or some-thing. I don't think she's very serious about it. In fact, she's totally irresponsible about most things.'

I'd never even met Carol but I was beginning to warm to her.

'She's been staying with me for the last two weeks. Oh, we always kept in touch, although she usually called to borrow money or clothes or when she was bumming around London and needed a bath or a bed. Anyway, this time she stayed longer than usual and it got a little tense towards the end. Last night, we got on each other's nerves worse than usual and I said something to the effect that I wished she'd piss off out of my lifestyle if all she wanted to do was bitch about it.'

'And you were disappointed when she did just that?'

Jo stared down at her electric-blue shoes and smiled at them.

'Well, I was surprised, I'll say that. She actually went and did it after threatening to at least a dozen times.'

'When did you find out?'

'About two in the morning. I couldn't sleep and thought I'd make a pot of tea, maybe offer Carol some ... you know ... peace offering. And there she was – gone. Along with a leather jacket, a bottle of vodka, my credit cards, some make-up and about 30 quid in cash.'

'And you want me to get your make-up back, huh?'

'There was also an emerald pendant. It was the only piece of jewellery she took but, true to form, she took the one thing that was most likely to hurt me.'

'Was it valuable?'

'About two and a half thousand pounds.'

'Is it insured?'

'No.' She shook her head slowly.

'Do you think this ... Carol ... will try and hock it?'

'No.' She was staring at her shoes again. 'Carol has no real idea about how much things are worth. Money and property mean nothing to her.'

'She took your credit cards and 30 quid,' I reminded her.

'The credit cards I've reported lost already, though I'll bet she's flushed them down the loo out of spite. I'll be surprised if she tried to use them. The cash will keep her in drinks and smokes for a couple of days, and good luck to her. It's only the pendant I want back. I must have it back – for sentimental reasons – and I don't care what happens to Carol.'

'That's not true, or you'd have called the cops.' She nodded silently. 'So why didn't you?'

'She's got what she calls "previous"; a couple of suspended sentences for shoplifting and a conviction for assault.'

'Assault?' I was going off Carol; rapidly.

'On a police horse during a student union demonstration.'

'Well, she could hardly expect a fair trial after that,' I said, not kidding. Let's face it, there are some crimes no-one should have to face the animal-loving British jury with.

'I don't want the police involved; well, not by me. If she brings them herself, that's her lookout. I don't want anything to do with her any more. I just want my pendant back.' For a second, her bottom lip jutted like a child's.

'Okay, I can relate to that, but why me?'

I mean, this wasn't my normal line of work, but why worry? She'd as good as said there would be a few quid in it.

'Because I saw you last night and because I couldn't think of any other single person to turn to. Have you ever been in that situation? Having nobody, nobody at all to go to? Jesus Christ, I couldn't tell my husband, could I? He gave me the fucking pendant.'

It was time to worry.

Of course, looking back, it was time to say goodbye, walk out of there and get on the first available Greenpeace boat heading for New Zealand. It would have been safer.

She didn't tell me much more – then. Yes, she did have a husband, and why should I be so shocked? (I couldn't really think why I should be either, except on the old hurt pride angle. I mean to say, the lover is always the last to know, isn't he?) Hubby was older, much older, than her and he was away a lot. Didn't I just know. He had splashed out on the emerald pendant for her 21st birthday and she had another birthday coming up. He would expect her to wear it then, and if he knew Carol had half-inched it, he would have the law on her without a second thought. It was worth ten percent – £250 – to her to have it back within a fortnight. Hubby would never twig it had gone walkies.

As I steered Armstrong back to Limehouse to pick up Frank's sander, I did wonder why Jo had refused to leave Champnas with me even though they seemed to have finished tweaking her hair into shape. Then I thought of 250 reasons why finding the girl drummer from Peking and then Carol and then the pendant would be a piece of cake. But just in case this Carol person mistook me for a police horse, it might be an idea to take Dod's 16 stone along for moral support.

Which made me think of where I'd heard this scenario before, the having the jewels back before the damsel in distress was put into a compromising position. Of course, it was the Queen's Diamonds in *The Three Musketeers*.

Shit. There were four of them on that job

CHAPTER FOUR

Lloyd Allen was my first connection, as he was supposed to be Peking's manager, or so Bill Stubbly had said.

I had thought about ringing Bill, but he was such an old woman I just couldn't face it. Lloyd would deal straight with me and he owed me a favour or two, mostly to do with unofficial deliveries of Red Stripe lager to unlicensed West Indian drinking dens that no one except the police, BBC documentary film crews and the entire West Indian community knew about.

Trying to track Lloyd down by night, unless you had a homing device on him, would be impossible, but I knew he shared an office in Curtain Road that I could try in the morning. So for the rest of that evening, I let Frank and Salome treat me to an additive-free, meat-less and fairly tasteless meal at a vegan wine bar they'd discovered in Southwark. Fortunately, Frank was in a mood to impress and lashed out on more white Bordeaux than he would have normally. With both of them watching their waistlines, I had to do the decent thing and drink most of it, and while I have a pretty good head for white wine (though not, oddly, for red, which is why I prefer red), I have to admit that Armstrong weaved slightly as we turned into Stuart Street and liberated the parking space nearest to No 9.

I was on a first-back-puts-the-coffee-on promise, so I was fiddling with filter papers when there was a knock on the flat door and I yelled, 'It's open.'

To my surprise, it was Lisabeth from the flat below. I've always maintained that Lisabeth stopped buying clothes in 1974. In fact, she's probably never bought anything except at jumble sales since then and lives in a late-hippie timewarp. I've even known her to wear bells when she's being going somewhere special, though that's rare. I think she had been a secretary somewhere along the line, but no-one seemed to know much about her. She took in typing for a living, rarely leaving the house and getting 'Binky' to run her errands. Maybe she was self-conscious about her size, but I don't see why she should be. Sea-lions aren't.

'Hello, Angel, glad I caught you.'

When the day comes when Lisabeth catches you, God help you.

'Hi. I'm just brewing up for Frank and Sal. Do you fancy a cup?'

'No, thanks, not stopping, wanted a favour.' I'd never noticed how talking to a male upset Lisabeth's speech pattern. 'Next week.'

'If it is in my power, my dear, you have but to command.' That was gallant enough and without double entendres. You have to be careful with Lisabeth. Frank Bruno would have to be careful with Lisabeth.

'I want to move in here for a few days,' she said, looking me straight in the eyes.

I wasn't shocked. I've been around, it's happened before. But Lisabeth? I decided I could pick up the coffee later.

'It's because of Bin ... Fenella.'

'You've had a fight?' I must have sounded incredulous, but the thought of Fenella standing up to this Amazon was just that.

'Good God no!' Lisabeth roared. 'Nothing like that. It's her parents, they're coming up from Rye for a few days and they ... they don't know about me ... us.'

I looked down at the floor as if considering it heavily.

'Are you telling me that we are really going to have the Binkworthys of Rye in this house – this very house?'

Lisabeth's upper lip began to curl. She was not the best person to try and wind-up.

'I'm sure we can work something out,' I said quickly. 'But you'll have to be nice to Springsteen.'

'It's a deal.' She smiled and turned on her heel. Without looking back she said: 'Do you mind him peeing in your coffee?'

Lloyd shared an office with a small record-sleeve-design company called Boot-In Inc. On the top floor of what seemed to be an otherwise deserted four-storey building in Curtain Road on the other side of the railway tracks that feed Liverpool Street station. Having cruised the area to find it, I could understand why Boot-In Inc had invested in a triple lock on their office door and a padlock and hasp big enough to have been nicked from Windsor Castle on the street door. Somebody was opening up as I arrived just after 10.00 am; the sort of office hours that could tempt me back into the rat race.

It was a white guy with long, black hair and a short, thick beard. He was taller and broader than me and running to the sort of fat that comes from too many hamburgers. He was carrying a parcel under one arm while struggling with the padlock. He was wearing white Kickers, white Levi's and a green nylon bomber jacket with 'Porsche' embroidered over the left tit. There was a six-year-old Hillman Avenger parked at the kerb.

We recognised each other. Maybe we'd gatecrashed the same party once.

'Angel, isn't it?' he said.

'Yeah. I'm looking for Lloyd. It's Danny, isn't it? Danny Boot.'

'If you're a friend of Lloyd's, it's Mr Boot

to you.' He did not smile when he said it. I remembered that about him. He never smiled.

'Give me a hand and you can come on up. Lloyd checks in about 11.00.' He gave me the parcel to hold while he worked on the padlock, and then added: 'Sometimes.'

The parcel was bulky but not heavy and about 18 inches square. It was wrapped in strong, brown paper and had a label with Boot's name on it and underneath simply: 'London Heathrow'. He got the front door open and led the way up a narrow flight of uncarpeted stairs, leaving me to carry the parcel.

'If this is prime-cut Colombian snow and the Drugs Squad are photographing us from that Avenger, I'll never forgive you.'

Boot snorted and stared up the second flight.

'They're videos, if you really must know.'

'Oh, I must, I must,' I smarmed.

'Okay. They're tapes of this week's MTV broadcasts from the States, flown in this morning. I've just collected them from Thiefrow. I get them sent by door-to-door courier.' He looked at me as if I'd just come up from the country and the mud hadn't dried on my wellies. 'All the airlines do it, you know. It costs about 30 quid and the stuff comes as cabin baggage with one of the hostesses. It's rarely checked by Customs, and if the plane gets here, so does your parcel. All dead straight, no naughties involved, perfectly legal. And anyway, the clapped-out old Avenger's mine.'

'What about taping the shows?'

'I didn't, did I? It was a guy over there did that. Of course, when I copy them and sell them up West in all the poseur café-bars, that's illegal. Oh yes.'

He would go far, would Boot. And his friends could always see him on visiting days.

Boot-In Inc, up another flight of stairs and through the triple-lock door, was one large, open-plan office containing half-a-dozen desks, several designer's easels, a couple of typewriters and a variety of video-recorders, amps, decks, tape-decks and speakers all spread carelessly across a red metal shelving unit that still had its Habitat price tag on. The office hadn't yet got to the word-processor and rented potted plants stage, but it would. Still, there was a good five grand's worth of gear there if you counted the mobile phones I also spotted. Not that it was really any of my business, of course, but it probably was insured…

There was also a coffee machine, which Boot ordered me to crank into action while he started making calls on one, and some-times two, of the mobile phones. I put him down as a phonoholic – he probably never had one as a child – for all he did while I was there was ring people. He didn't say much to them after 'Hello,' he just grunted a lot.

Staff drifted in and sat down at various workstations, though not many of them made any obvious effort to work. Mostly they found a spare phone and rang people up. Their mothers, their bookmakers, even a bank manager or two. One even rang the speaking clock just to feel part of the crowd. Maybe Boot had bought into Telecom shares.

Being the only one not phoning anybody, I was the only one who heard Lloyd, though it was a good five minutes before I saw him.

I didn't identify the music until he was probably half-way up the stairs, and even then I had to listen carefully before plumping for 'Riverside Stomp', a Johnny Dankworth (sorry, John Dankworth) piece from a British B picture called *The Criminal*. (Directed by Joseph Losey in 1960 and starring Stanley Baker and Sam Wanamaker. Dankworth played alto and Dudley Moore played piano, if you ever need to know.)

I'd forgotten that Lloyd was deeply into the whole *Absolute Beginners* scene, from drainpipe shiny Italian suits (nowadays made in Bulgaria) and bootlace ties to driving around in an ancient yellow Triumph Herald coupé. So not everything was absolutely authentic, but you know how difficult it is to

67

pick up an original Bubble Car these days? Fashions change, though, and I predict a rush on the old Fiat 500s any day now. As soon as I get some cash, I'm cornering the market, which is something the Fiats never did. The other anachronism with Lloyd, of course, was the portable stereo clamped to his shoulder. Now I know that the old Ferranti Gramophone would hardly be practical let alone smart, but in truth I don't think anything would separate Lloyd from his Brixton briefcase.

To give him his due, he did turn the noise level down to a dull roar as he entered the office. 'Well, hello one and all,' he beamed. 'And Angel-my-man, it's you himself.'

'The one and only. How's the wrestling business?'

'More coin there than the music business, my man, and–' he looked around the office – 'you get to meet a nicer class of person. But I'm a specialist, man. Female wrestlers only, and only in mud.'

Boot managed to put down a phone for a minute and ambled over to us holding an artwork board.

'Your record cover, Mr Allen,' he said. Then to me: 'See how polite I can be when this pimpy poseur owes us money?'

Lloyd flipped the cover sheet back and looked at the design, then showed it to me. It was a sepia tint of the Great Wall of China with the faces of the three members of the group Peking superimposed at intervals as if carved into the stone. In small, Chinese-style characters down one side was the album's title: '55 Days'. You could have guessed.

'That's large, man, really large,' breathed Lloyd like a proud parent. 'What do you make of it, Mr A?'

'Awesome, Lloyd, really awesome.'

Lloyd's clothes may be 1960 Soho, but his jive was pure Malibu surf talk. 'Large' was the word of the year, rapidly replacing 'awesome,' which had ousted 'outstanding' around 1985. I've always found, though, when dealing with someone like Lloyd, that it pays to let him be one step ahead – if, that is, you want something from him.

'So, you've got a record contract for them. Hey, that's really great, man. It's about them I wanted…'

'Hey, don't be too previous. Who said anything about a contract?'

Boot parked his bum on the edge of a desk and put on his Sunday-best sneer.

'Lloyd does it the easy way, didn't you know? Gets an album cover, gets a fan club, gets some T-shirts and then plays one recording company off against another. It helps if the band can play, but it's not essential.' That was quite a speech for Boot.

'Someday I'm going to do it without a band,' grinned Lloyd.

'And give us decent entrepreneurs a bad name,' said Boot, dead serious, though a less likely disciple of Milton Friedman I couldn't think of. 'Which is why I'll take cash for this job. No more percentages. Two percent of nothing is fuck-all.'

'Okay, so give me a bill, Mr B.' Lloyd's face lit up. 'Hey! Mr A and Mr B. What do you know!'

'And we all know who Mr C is,' said Boot, leaning forward to pat Lloyd on the cheek. 'Don't go away, my man. I'll get you an invoice.'

'I think the cover is great, Lloyd,' I said as Boot moved away. 'And the band is good. I played with them the other night at the Mimosa.'

'Oh yeah.' Lloyd was looking at his band's album cover, not too aware of me.

'That's why I wanted to see you,' I pushed on. 'It's the girl drummer. I need to contact her.'

'Emma? What you want with her?'

'Yeah, Emma. I'm looking for a friend of hers and she might know where she is.'

Lloyd looked up. 'You got the hots for Emma or something?'

'No, straight up, nothing like that.' Well, that was honest enough. 'It's a friend of hers I'm after. I just need to talk to her.'

'Well, okay, Mr A, I'll trust you, 'cos you're not the man to jive old Lloyd here, but you'd better not hassle my protégée.' He pronounced it pro-tay-jay. 'She's at a very delicate stage of her development, man, and I don't want the little lady upset.'

'She's writing songs, huh? Talented lady.'

'Hell no,' laughed Lloyd. 'She's doing her O-levels.'

About the only thing Hampstead and Hackney share in common is a dropped aitch. Even the pubs in Hampstead are different, being mostly Italian restaurants that accidentally sell beer if you have the required amount of readies, which in some cases meant an Amex card had to do nicely thank you.

The address Lloyd gave me was impressive. I'm not giving it here because Emma's father slipped me a few of the folding to keep his secret now that Emma's getting well-known in the music business. Not her secret, you note: his. He doesn't want the neighbours to know.

Anyway, the house was a big, Georgian affair that Daddy probably afforded on a two percent mortgage from the bank he worked for. It took me a while, though, before I realised that Daddy owned all of it. I'd assumed at first that the place would be carved up into flats.

I had a bit of trouble finding a suitable parking space for Armstrong (Rule 177) among the Metro Citys and those ubiquitous VW Golfs, which I'm sure are breeding somewhere in the backstreets, but I'd sussed the right house, and so it was down to a frontal attack up the six wide stone steps to the door and doing something dynamic like ringing the doorbell. The sound of drums from somewhere up above met me half-way. So she was in. I was rehearsing a line like 'Hello, is Carol coming out to play?' and trying to improve on it when the drumming stopped to be replaced by footsteps in the hallway.

You must have seen the old horror films where the hero or heroine knocks on the door of the isolated, spooky house ('completely cut off at high tide, young master...') seeking shelter from the storm. You hear the clump of footsteps for ages before at least 60 bolts are drawn or locks turned and then Karloff's skull peers round the door edge and he says: 'I'm thorry I took tho long, thir, but I wath delayed at my devotionth.' There is also the spoof version – though nobody spoofed Karloff better than Karloff – where the footsteps are really loud and echoing and then the gaunt butler eventually appears wearing carpet slippers.

If either had happened, it couldn't have surprised me more.

The door opened and there was a 15-year-old schoolgirl in regulation grey pullover and knee-length pleated skirt, white, knee-length socks, sensible shoes and white shirt with a tie tied with a better knot than I could ever manage.

When times have been hard and the cash-flow not flowing, I have been known (though not by my friends) to take orchestra-pit work in some of the provincial theatres not too hot on Musicians' Union membership. But in all the tacky pantomime transformation scenes I'd witnessed, and you get a pretty good view from the pit, none had anything on Emma. The make-up and black nail polish could all come off easily, of course, and the clothes made an enormous difference, but it was the hair that she had worked wonders with. The salmon-pink colouring could have been just vegetable dye and easily washed out, but where had the Mohican cut gone? It took me a few seconds to work out that she'd shaved the sides of her head but had left enough length in her mousy locks to be able to comb it flat and round and into a short pony tail held at the back with an elastic band. As both schoolgirl and punk she must get through a gallon of hair gel a week to keep it in place.

'Yes?' she said before I could think of anything remotely amusing.

Even then, all I got out was, 'Er, hi! I'm from the Mimosa...' before she cut in.

'If you're another one of Stubbly's goons,

you can just piss off back to that dungheap of his. I had more than enough of that place the other night. I wondered how long it would be before he tried a shakedown.' She looked me in the eye. 'Tell him to get off my case.'

She began to close the door, so I put my right foot in the way, and when she saw that she pulled the door back, but only to get a better swing and more weight behind it.

'Hang about, darling, I was in the band with you. I'm Angel, the trumpet man.'

The door stopped an inch from my trainers.

'Shouldn't that be Gabriel?' she said.

'Oh, very sharp, get in the knife drawer.' The door moved again. 'It really is my name. And anyway, Stubbly doesn't employ goons,' I finished quickly, to give her something to think about.

'Well, he bloody well had a tame gorilla in tow the other night. You might have gone by then, though. Yeah, you had.'

'So, what was the problem?'

'Oh, just Stubbly being an old fart. He came into the back room late on. I was waiting for Geoff to take me home. He's the one who went off to find our so-called manager Lloyd with that sex-starved saxophone player. He's a friend of yours, isn't he?'

I admitted that the description might just fit somebody I knew called Bunny, but I hadn't seen him in years. Well, Tuesday.

'Do you think we could go inside?' I asked. 'I think I'm upsetting the au-pair-owning classes. I could have sworn I heard a net curtain twitch.'

'Don't be daft,' said Emma, not smiling. 'You could set off a bomb round here and not wake the zombies, but try clamping a car and it's Return of the Living Dead.'

I knew what she meant. London had just lived through its first summer of wheel-clamping illegally parked cars, and fear and paranoia now stalked the double yellow lines. Businessmen had hired chauffeurs by the herd to keep fleets of limos constantly on the move going round the one-way systems while they were at meetings. I put it down to a conspiracy between the oil companies and the Government to keep petrol sales up and create jobs at the same time.

'Well, you can come in and watch me eat lunch,' she relented. 'But another slagging-off from the older generation I don't need.'

I didn't move and must have looked hurt.

'Oh, be fair,' she said, 'you are old enough to be my father, aren't you?'

'Was your mother in Norwich in the spring of 1971?'

'Not that I know of.'

'Then I think we're safe.'

She led me down a hallway I could have driven Armstrong through and into a kitchen bigger than my flat. It had a long pine table around which you could have sat a platoon of hungry infantrymen, and two pine Welsh dressers made from reconditioned tea-chests (which are gold dust these days), groaning with Le Creuset ovenware and Jocelyn Dimbleby cookbooks.

Emma produced a granary loaf and a bread knife, then a jar of peanut butter. Another bloody vegan.

'Got to eat,' she said, 'I've got an exam this afternoon. Got an oily on yer?'

'Oily' – oily rag – fag – cigarette. The exam was obviously English O-level. I produced one.

'They ain't got roaches,' she complained. Maybe it was A-level.

'Life's like that.' I offered a light. 'So what was the aggro at the Mimosa? Stubbly catch you dropping something?'

'Sort of.' She stood at the table spreading peanut butter with the bread knife on a slice of wholemeal the shape of one of those chocks you stick under a barrel of beer. The cigarette drooped from the corner of her mouth as if it had all the cares of the world bearing down on it.

'Bill doesn't like drugs, you know. Somebody should have told you.'

Ever since she'd said 'shakedown' I'd guessed it was drugs. It had to be either drugs or sex, and in her after-dark punk persona, she was pretty passé for Soho these days. Not, mind you, that she couldn't have done a good trade in Shepherd's Market on the telephone circuits run from the bank of call-boxes at King's Cross. (You must have seen the adverts on white adhesive labels that have gone up all over town. 'Tall black model needs discipline'; 'Young and petite interested in clothing exchange'; and so on.)

'Yeah, well, that became bloody obvious.'

'So what were you doing?' I tried not to make it a father's Oh-not-again-Emma sort of voice.

'I was just about to snort a line, if you must know. Just a small line of low-grade. Well, I was pissed off waiting with only the toilet for company. Stubbly came in and went apeshit, but it wasn't so much that – that I can handle – but it was the other guy with him being mad at him. Like he was very disappointed with Stubbly, you know, a quiet sort of mad that means you're going to get it in the neck at some future date.'

'Who was this guy?'

'Like I said, he was a goon. A gorilla, regular Management. A bouncer, you know, somebody who breaks Tonka toys for a living.'

'Big guy?'

'Like a brick shithouse. Blocked out the natural light for miles.'

'Have a name?'

'Would you believe Nevil? Bit of a poncy name for a thug that size. Yeah, Nevil. Well, that's what Stubbly kept calling him. And all he kept saying was: "This isn't good enough, he won't like it" – saying it to Stubbly, that is.'

'What did he say to you?'

'Just "Out" and pointed to the door, but Stubbly was a right pair of nun's knickers.'

'Pardon?'

'Nun's knickers – always on. And on and on. Never darken door again, all that stuff. Sod him. That's why I thought you were coming to put the squeeze on Daddy.'

I saw her bite her tongue as 'Daddy' slipped out.

'As if I looked the sort,' I said, trying to work out how to put the squeeze on Stubbly. 'No, I came for a favour.'

'Here we go,' sighed Emma, rolling her eyes to the ceiling.

'No, straight up. I'm looking for Carol, your mate.'

'Flaxperson?' I must have looked dumb. 'Carol's surname is Flaxman, you wally, but she's a feminist. Daddy doesn't like her.'

'So she's not staying here?' I asked quickly to help her gloss over the second 'Daddy'.

'No, she's gone back to university.'

'When?'

'Yesterday morning. She rang me about 6.00 am. She was well pissed. Said she'd loved the band and was sorry she hadn't seen me after the set. Said she had to get back to the front line now the weather was getting better, and was catching the first train from Liverpool Street. Typical Carol. Six o'clock in the bleeding morning. I'd only just got in. Woke the whole house.'

'I know the feeling,' I muttered. 'What did she mean by "front line"?'

Emma shrugged. 'University? Going back to her lectures or something? I'm going to have to get back to school myself.'

'Can I give you a lift?'

She looked me up and down, and I could tell she was trying to work out the kudos value of arriving with me in front of her friends.

'Okay, it's not far.' She picked up a pencil case made out of a soft toy and a zip. It resembled a wombat that had been in a car accident.

'What did you want with Flaxperson anyway?'

Well, I think that's what she said but it was difficult to tell as she had pushed the last of the peanut butter into her mouth. She chewed and wiggled her pleats down the hallway in front of me.

'She borrowed some tapes from a friend of mine and I need them,' I mumbled, and fortunately she didn't seem interested.

'She'll have flogged them by now, knowing

her,' said Emma sagely. 'I once caught her negotiating to sell my drum kit.'

'Do you ever need to get in touch with her?' I asked innocently.

'Nah, no chance. Flaxperson finds you. Usually when you least want her to.'

We were out on the steps now.

'Though I suppose Essex University would know where she hangs out. Bet she owes them money.'

'Who doesn't?' I made to unlock Armstrong.

'You drive that?' shrieked Emma, taking a pace back.

'My Porsche is having its ashtrays emptied,' I said, getting upset. After all, Armstrong had been insulted by professionals.

'Well, I'm not turning up at school in that thing. People will think I'm only allowed out under guard. They'll think Daddy sent you. I'll walk.'

She primped past me down the pavement.

'I hope the skinheads get yer!' I yelled after her. But I hoped for their sake they didn't.

CHAPTER FIVE

I pointed Armstrong towards Regent's Park, but after Chalk Farm I cut through to Islington and down York Way to the Waterside Inn.

I decided on the Waterside because it had a phone, beer you couldn't get anywhere else in London and a very interesting turnover in young French female chefs. (The French, being Socialist, have to train girls to cook, but being chauvinists, only let males do it for real. Hence considerable numbers of chefesses willing to come over here and work for peanuts just for the experience. Some of them get to cook as well.)

There was another advantage late on a lunch-time in that there were always a few city slickers who had ventured north by north-west (of the Barbican) to try the Hoskin's or the Holden's bitter and found it had got the better of them, so needed a taxi back to civilization.

It was young and shy Nadine on duty, so I got a large portion of chicken in white wine sauce with rice (how is it that the French can cook rice that never sticks?) and a bottle of Pils for next to nothing. As I made inroads into both, I sussed the other punters, and though the place was fairly quiet, there were a couple of city gents in suits talking earnestly and drinking fast. Just the sort who didn't work locally and who would need a ride back to the office, come chucking-out time at three. It was a good hunting ground in the summer, as the front of the pub overlooked the basin that served as the headquarters of London's trendy and ever-growing population of canal boats. It was only a matter of time, though, before the pub won the *Standard* Pub of the Year Award, and after that it would be all downhill.

I risked another Pils. I'm usually quite abstemious during daylight hours if I have any driving to do. After all, I don't want to lose any of my licences, do I? Then I sorted out some ten ps for the phone and rifled through my diary (*The Sex Maniac's Diary* – it was a Christmas present, not my idea) for Jo's number.

She must have been sitting over the phone.

'Yes?'

'It's me, Angel.'

'Oh hello, Celia,' she said, and I knew instantly that something was wrong. I'm quick like that.

'There's somebody with you, isn't there?'

'That's absolutely right, Celia, I never could fool you. Now tell me all your news.'

It was a good act and almost convinced me, but in situations like this, there's nothing to do except play along.

'I'll be brief,' I said, businesslike. 'Carol's split town and gone back to university as far as anyone knows. Last reported early yesterday morning, high as a kite, heading for a train. Sorry.'

'Well, why don't you go too, Celia?' she came back, totally unfazed. 'After all, if it's worth so much to you, you could be there and back in a day easily.'

Just like that. Some nerve, and of course I went for it.

'If I did, how the hell do I find her and how do I make her part with your pendant?' From what I'd heard of La Flaxperson, a crowbar might help. Jo certainly wasn't going to.

'Well, you could always try one of those women's groups, dear. I hear they're very popular. And don't worry about the child. They always see sense in the end. I don't think you'll have any trouble.'

'Okay, then, I'll give it a go if you'll pay for the diesel and if I can see you Saturday night.'

'What's on on Saturday?'

'Party night. I'll give you a ring around lunch-time.'

'I'll have to see about that, Celia, but it sounds a nice idea. Talk to you tomorrow.'

She hung up, leaving me thinking that if she wasn't actually a spy, she was wasted. But then, what was she?

I finished my lager and walked outside to wind up Armstrong. I'd just turned on to York Way when I spotted the two city gents who'd been drinking in the pub. One of them hailed me and gave me a fiver to take them to a private clinic in Harley Street. On the way, they shared from a silver hip flask. Thank God there was still the National Health.

And so, despite all my years of philosophical training (Rule of Life No 2: don't be a mug) and against all my better judgments (Judgments in question, on a scale of 0-ten: 0), I went. Not that I minded the actual going, as it were. It was the heavy scene that followed that was the problem.

To anyone who hasn't been to, taught at or scrounged off, a modern university, the prospect of tracking somebody down with basically only a name to go on must sound daunting. It's a piece of piss really, if you have a few clues. I'm not bragging, but by the time I really started to look for Carol Flaxman, I knew it would be a matter of hours rather than days.

Well, look at it from my point of view. I knew she was registered at Essex, I knew she was basically dishonest, a boozer, a feminist and – from the brief glimpse I'd caught of her in the Mimosa Club – featherweight. Okay, so I was looking for a politically active, fat, drunk kleptomaniac. There couldn't be that many around. I mean, Essex only has 3,000 students on a good day, and modern university campuses may be foreign turf to you, but they're happy hunting grounds to people like me.

But like all good hunters going into the jungle, I needed camouflage. Armstrong was too clichéd to be a student vehicle these days, unless it was a London-based medical student; they are well-known to be from another planet ten years behind the times. So first priority was to find a vehicle not out of place at somewhere like Essex.

What do students drive these days? In my day we had taxis or Beetles or the old-style Escorts, and Australians always had VW Dormobiles. (You can still buy one cheap in the car park round the corner from Victoria, as they're auctioned off by young Ozzers looking for the fare home.) Knowing my luck, they'd all be driving Golfs or Saabs with green windscreen visors with their names – Tarquin and Petra – on them.

I settled for convenience and anonymity. What I needed was something like a slightly battered Ford Transit van, and I knew exactly where I could borrow one.

The early evening rush-hour slowed my

return to Stuart Street, but I was still the first home to No 9, and even Lisabeth seemed to be out or at least locked in her cage. I used the privacy to make some calls on the house phone without logging them in the red exercise book Mr Goodson had drawing-pinned to the wall. The first was to Duncan the Drunken in Barking, who agreed to do me a weekend deal on a Transit in exchange for a loan of Armstrong. I agreed and arranged to pick it up the next morning on the way.

The second call was to someone else and necessitated me going out later that night to pick up two ounces of best Lebanese Red and three of mixed grass and seed, on a sale-or-return basis.

I do have some scruples, though. I refused this week's special offer of £15 Lucky Bags of H (probably cut with arrowroot) point blank.

Duncan the Drunken ran a small lock-up garage off Longbridge Road in Barking, and he and the wife, Doreen, lived in a two-up-two-down round the corner. I say 'the wife' with impunity as Doreen is one of the few wives I know who actually calls herself that. Some marriages are made in heaven, but Duncan's and Doreen's was forged in Sheffield. She was one of the last of the anachronistic breed of Northern women who only spoke to men when spoken to, or after three port and lemons, whichever came first. Yes, she was also the only woman since Freddie and the Dreamers had a hit who still drank port and lemon.

Why Duncan and Doreen had come to London in the mid '70s, and why they stayed, was a mystery. Duncan had been appalled to find that women had the vote 'down South,' and had got off to a shaky start in the motor trade when one of the local spivs conned him into thinking a Pina Colada was the latest model Ford built in Spain. In ten years, he had alienated his neighbours (all races and ethnic minorities offended equally) by playing the nosey, over-matey Yorkshireman to excess. Now the area was being done up by the young middle class, he stubbornly refused to paint his house and remained firmly working class to the extent of asking the Council to bring back his outside toilet. All his attempts to organise street parties, coach outings and singalongs in the local pubs ended in abject failure. Yet he remained disgustingly cheerful and unputdownable, and his capacity for what he called warm, flat, sloppy Southern beer was legendary.

Duncan had his head inside the engine of a rather tasty BMW. The registration plates said it was only two years old, but I stopped believing registration plates about two years before I gave up waiting for the tooth fairy.

'Ah've come for mah van, Duncan,' I drawled from the garage doorway.

'Well, I nivver thought I'd catch you up and about at sparrowfart, young Angel.'

Duncan straightened up and tucked a wrench into the leg pocket of his dungarees. 'Cuppa char?'

'Why not?' I might as well; there was bargaining to be done, and so the ritual had to be observed.

As the pubs weren't open yet, this meant a brew-up in the little office annexe at the back of the garage. I could tell from the amount of condensed milk that Duncan dripped into his Queen's Jubilee china mug that he had a hangover.

We all have our pet remedies and recipes. I have two, one (a pint of ice-cold Gold Top milk – not for the faint of stomach) based on a need for nourishment and the other (about a pint of tonic water over lots of ice and Angostura bitters) to combat dehydration and that ashtray mouth feeling.

Duncan must have followed my thought-train.

'So what do you reckon's good for a hangover, then?'

'Well, drinking heavily the night before usually works for me,' I said, pinching an old Ben Elton line.

'We supped some stuff last night, I can tell

you.' Duncan handed me a cracked Royal Wedding souvenir mug. He was nothing if not patriotic – that is, he drank only at pubs called the Queen's Head or Arms.

'Any particular cause for celebration?' I asked, to pass the time until the tea cooled.

'It was Thursday.'

'Fair enough. How's Doreen?'

'Champion, lad, champion. Started going to night school. Think she needs an interest now the kids are growing up.'

'That's nice. What's she taking – cookery?' Doreen's cooking was notoriously bad.

'No, that's what I wanted her to do, but she's got her own mind now.' I wondered where she'd found one, but I said nothing. 'She's gone for panel beating and auto mechanics.'

'You'll be out of a job soon.'

'Nivver, lad. I was on the dole in Sheffield once and I swore I'd sweep streets rather than going back.'

I wasn't sure whether he meant to Sheffield or the dole. Maybe both. I glanced towards the garage entrance, which was ankle deep in litter.

'The street needs sweeping, Duncan. Set up a company and get the Council to privatise the refuse collection.'

'It's a thought, Angel, lad, it's a thought.'

'Does this mean you've got me a dustbin van?'

'No. Could've done if you'd wanted one, though.' He slurped the last of his tea. 'I stuck to me brief, as the Archbishop said in court. You wanted a Transit, I got one. Took it in part exchange last week, and I've got a buyer coming Wednesday, so I want it back in one piece. It's out back.'

As he led me through the back door and onto the waste ground he used as an un-official parking lot, he said: 'Good runner, only 30,000 on the clock.'

'How many on the engine?' I asked.

'Oh about 115,000, but only 30 on the clock. There's a problem, though.'

Other people say 'Yes, but...' Duncan used 'though' in the same way.

'It's left-hand drive.'

In fact, it was not only left-hand drive, it had German number plates, a hefty dent in the nearside panel, a window sticker saying 'Stop the Bloody Whaling' and a bumper sticker saying 'Nein Danke' to nuclear power, and the whole thing had been garishly resprayed in two-tone brown and purple.

'Duncan,' I said, 'it's perfect.'

Like a lot of modern universities, you get into Essex one of two ways – from the side or underneath. The campus buildings are based around five squares raised on concrete stilts, which were officially known as podia. The architect had got the idea from the piazzas of small towns in northern Italy. What he hadn't counted on was the tunnel effect of putting five together and pointing them into a wind that came more or less straight from the Urals after turning left over Norway. That and the rain, which stained the concrete dirty brown, gave the place a deserted look even during term-time; but the fact that it was so close to London meant that it really was deserted at the weekends as students and staff headed for the bright lights.

It was just after noon on a Friday when I arrived, so the weekend exodus was just starting. I parked the van in one of the perimeter car parks and walked through the campus buildings reading the graffiti until I saw the amended sign reading 'Stundent Onion,' and one that hadn't been vandalised saying simply 'Bar.'

Most of the Students' Union offices seemed to be below square level, under the podia. As the floor-numbering system at all modern universities is totally unintelligible to everyone except the drug-crazed mathematician who thought it up, I just followed my nose.

There's something about student bars, mostly the smell, that you never get in even the roughest pub. I rarely used them when I was a legitimate student, much preferring the local pubs. They always had uncleanable carpets and too few ashtrays (prime targets for students living in halls of residence) and the service is usually lousy. In recent years, they've all got the real ale kick and always have too many pumps, which means that the throughput is slow and four out of five beers go off before they're half sold.

I bypassed the bar, which was slowly filling with shuffling students, and read a Letrasetted sign: 'Union Print Room – Affiliated to National Graphical Association (Pending).' The door it adorned was open, and inside came the familiar sound of a photocopier on print and collate.

The guy operating the machine seemed a likely touch. He was about my age (though he looked it) but taller and stringier than me, and he had a close-cropped beard but no moustache, which is usually a bad sign. (Rule of Life No 81: never trust a man with a beard but a naked upper lip – he's either a sociologist or a religious fanatic.) The rest of him, though, ran true to form: an old school blazer, jeans so faded they could appear in a Levi's ad any day now, and what appeared to be a genuine, official Born To Run tour T-shirt. There you had it, the archetypal should-know-better-at-his-age professional student. You'll find them all over the country. They nearly always end up in local government or the probation service. (Rule of Life No 307: when a student, remember – the comrade on the march today is the police chief of tomorrow.)

'Need a hand?' I asked, knowing that his type just couldn't wait to get you *involved*.

'Can you use a stapler?'

'Do I get a retraining grant?'

'We don't make jokes at the expense of the unemployed.'

My God, if he wasn't the genuine article! I didn't think they bred them like that any more. Still, it's nice to know some things hardly change.

'Why not? The Government does.'

He grinned and pointed to an electric stapler clamped to the edge of the table.

'They're all collated,' he said, reaching for another pack of paper. 'Clip them once, top left-hand corner, and stack 'em anywhere.'

He was running off some sort of three-page newsletter under a clenched-fist-wrapped-in-barbed-wire masthead. The articles were badly typed on at least three different machines and had headings like: 'Pretoria: Sanctions NOW!' and 'No Nukes Is Good Nukes.' I resisted the temptation to read more.

'Are you up for the weekend?' he asked.

'Yeah, flying visit. Does it show?' I was up-set. I thought I looked more like a student than he did.

'Nobody round here ever volunteers to help. You here for an interview or something?'

'Oh no. I've served my time already,

elsewhere. No, I'm looking for a friend.'

Young Trotsky finished his printing and began to pack the copies I had stapled into an old US Army haversack. In the bar upstairs, a juke-box started up loudly. Diana Ross's 'Chain Reaction' (nice video, shame about the song).

'Drive up?'

I nodded. 'How do I go about finding somebody here?'

'Do you know which school?'

'Social Studies, I think.' It seemed the best bet. There was bound to be one.

'You won't get any sense out of the School Office now.' He glanced at the Spiderman watch on his left wrist. 'Not after 12.00 on a Friday. And the porters will only leave a message in the piggyholes if she lives on campus. Did you say you had a car here?'

'No, I didn't say, and it's a van. I don't suppose you know her, do you? Carol Flax-man.'

He stroked his beard.

'Don't know her as such. Wasn't she one of the '84 Four?'

'The what?'

'The four who were suspended for a year in 1984 after the demos during the Miners' Strike. Is it a big van?'

'Big enough. Would that little demo have involved a slight incident with a police horse?'

94

'That's the one. Made all the papers.'

'And that sounds like the right Carol. I hear she's back now.'

'If she is, she won't be living on campus. None of them are, they're all persona-non-fucking-grata. Alan might know, of course. He was one of the Four suspended.'

'Can I get hold of this Alan easily?'

Young Trotsky smiled an impish smile. 'You wouldn't by chance be going into Colchester, would you?'

'As soon as I track down Carol, I'm free. You want a lift somewhere?'

'That'd be great. Alan's upstairs in the bar. He works as a potboy on Fridays, collecting glasses.'

'Shouldn't that be potperson?' I asked innocently.

'No, that means something completely different, though in Alan's case you might be right.'

He finished packing up his newsletters, and I followed him upstairs into the bar. A thin, gangling, blond guy was stalking the tables, emptying ashtrays into a battered wastepaper bin and snarling at the customers.

Young Trotsky said: 'Heh, Alan, there's a guy here wants a word,' and then proceeded to distribute his newsletter around the tables to a less-than-rapturous welcome from the patrons.

'If you're looking to buy, I've nothing to

sell,' said Alan for openers, as if he was at a jumble sale.

'I'm supplied. I'm told you can help me find an old friend, Carol Flaxman.'

'Says who?'

'He did.' I jerked a thumb at the amateur newspaper vendor.

'We call him Murdoch; he's our would-be press baron.' Alan banged another ashtray into the bin to make it look as if he was working. 'Yeah, I know where Flaxperson is; I saw her the other day. She tried to score off me and offered to pay by credit card.'

Now that's not uncommon in London these days, but then this was the sticks. I pretended to look shocked. 'Bet it wasn't hers, either.'

'Dead right. I see you know Carol.'

'Not well, but I'm not losing any sleep over that.'

He looked me up and down, not sure what to make of me. That put him on a par with most of the population, but I must have come up to his standards.

'She's on the front line,' he said, and it wasn't meant to be enigmatic.

'And where's that these days?'

'RAF Bentwaters in Suffolk, though I suppose you should call it USAF Bentwaters.'

'She's joined the Air Force?'

'More sort of the peace force sitting outside the perimeter wire singing folk songs and eating yoghurt.'

'Sounds awful.'

'It is, and if you go there you'll be lucky to escape with your balls.'

'I'm known as the Great Escaper. Which way to the front line?'

Alan showed me another way out of the bar, so we avoided Young Trotsky, and walked with me to the van. He showed me the location of Bentwaters in the old *AA Book of the Road* I always carried, and then bought the two ounces of Red from me at four times what I'd agreed to pay for it.

No day is wasted.

CHAPTER SIX

Before I rejoined the A12 northwards for Suffolk (okay, so it lacks the ring of 'North to Alaska!'), I called in at a Sainsbury's to buy some essential items. These comprised a pork pie and some salami to stave off the munchies while I drove, a toothbrush and some toothpaste, and then a bottle each of tequila, lime juice and Asti Spumante for which I had plans.

I had forgotten how beautiful the Suffolk countryside could be, even from a dual carriageway full of juggernauts from Holland and Denmark and Ford Escorts full of reps all with their coats hung neatly in the back and their Barry Manilow tapes belting out.

Bentwaters is, or was, an RAF base that had long been occupied by the American Air Force, probably since the War, proving the theory that East Anglia is the biggest non-floating US aircraft carrier in the world. The main entry road was well sealed off with roadblocks and white-helmeted military cops, behind which a little bit of American Mid-West flourished. Chilled PX Budweiser was drunk in preference to the local Adnams bitter, best mince was called 'ground beef' and the *East Anglian Daily Times* was bought only to find out what time the Bears were playing the Steelers on Channel 4.

Not that I've anything against Americans; far from it. I feel quite sorry for some of the airbase families, in fact. Since the revival of CND, many of them have thought twice about ever setting foot outside their bases. Well, can you blame them? So the base kids went to base schools and the base moms shopped at base shops and the base officers toured the base cocktail-party circuit. Occasionally some of the other ranks could be seen driving old Chevvies (they brought their own cars with them rather than risk going to local garages) with number plates proclaiming their owner to be from the Potato or Sunshine States or, ironically, from the Land of the Free.

The Front Line peace camp was not difficult to find, mainly because of the hundred or so handwritten signs (most on the back of crisp boxes) saying 'Front Line' with a badly drawn arrow, which had been threaded into the wire perimeter fence. I bet the MPs wished they had invested in electrification. More ominously, there were dozens of signs saying 'Ladies,' which at one time had adorned public loos.

The camp was actually down a farm track to one side of the base. The security at the main gate must have been too tight to let them get established, but tucked away around the perimeter fence they were less of an eyesore and small nuisance. Similarly, I suppose, the peace camp was more or less left in peace round there.

By Greenham standards, which must be the yardstick for these things, the camp was minute. There were about 20 tents and makeshift lean-tos in a semicircle spanning about 40 yards of the fence. Through the wire was an overgrown, obviously unused concrete runway and, far in the distance, the outlying buildings of the base. As far as the military were concerned, this was a good site for the camp, out of sight and far enough away from anything important.

As I eased the Transit over some of the more violent ruts in the track, I noticed that one of the lean-tos was in fact an old, single-decker bus from which the wheels had been removed. It lay tilted to one side, its body-work rusting into the ground. Its windows had been spray-painted in blues and reds, so that from a distance it looked as if the bus had curtains on the outside. Most the remaining paintwork was covered in CND symbols, as were most of the T-shirts, jeans, smock tops and even a couple of nappies that hung on a clothes line stretched between the bus and the fence. There seemed to be no sign of any transport that actually worked.

About 50 feet from the first tent, I turned the van around and pulled it slightly off the track. I could see in the wing mirror that my arrival had provoked some interest. About half a dozen women and children had appeared and were standing, holding hands, watching me. I felt like the cops arriving in the hippie camp in *Electra Glide in Blue* (the right-winger's *Easy Rider.)*

They were all dressed in about three sets of clothing, each of which they probably slept in, and all had the ingrained-grimy faces of people living without running water. I was glad I hadn't shaved that morning.

The eldest of the group who moved towards me as I jumped out of the van was no more than 30. She had thin, straggly, dirty-blonde rats-tail hair and wore wellingtons, faded pink jeans and a baggy knitted pullover with a row of pink pigs across the bosom. In her left hand she held the hand of a small child dressed in a raincoat at least eight sizes too big. In her right hand she weighed something that made a strange, metallic click-click sound.

It was a sound I hadn't heard since Manchester United played West Ham at Upton Park: ball-bearings – totally vicious and very effective at close range. These girls had learned a lot from their peace camp.

Rats-Tail stopped the group ten feet away,

and they fanned out in a semi-circle. I had the nasty feeling they'd done this before. The only other male in sight was about four years old and hadn't been potty-trained.

'It's too late now,' said Rats-Tail.

'Surely, it never is.' I turned on the smile. I have good teeth and they've been known to blind at five yards in strong sunlight. No response.

'It's too late,' said Rats-Tail again, with more hostility than petulance. 'So you might as well go.'

'Too late for what?' I took an involuntary step backwards nearer the van.

'To sign on,' said Rats-Tail, shaking her head in exasperation. 'Bloody woman!'

The others said nothing. One woman drifted away with a couple of the children as if she'd heard it all before.

'Bloody Carol!' spat Rats-Tail.

'Carol Flaxman?'

'Yes.' Suspicion now, but vitriol won out over loyalty. 'That selfish cow can't get anything right.'

'What's she done now?' I asked in a you-don't-have-to-tell-me-anything-about-Carol voice, with an I'm-on-your-side sort of sigh.

'That dopey mare left about five hours ago to find us some transport so we could all go into Ipswich and sign on. It's too late now, the DHSS will be shut and there's naff-all to eat in the camp except lentils.'

No wonder they were upset, relying on Flaxperson for their next social security Giro when down to their last lentil.

'I haven't seen her,' I said. 'But I want to; that's why I came. My name's Dave.'

The ball-bearings stopped clicking.

'I'm Melanie.' She nodded to the child at her side. 'This is Antiope.'

'Hello, Antiope,' I smiled. Poor kid. I thought I had trouble with names, but I wasn't going to ask, because I knew Antiope was the mother of Achilles in Greek mythology. Such are the benefits of a public school education.

'We can go look for her if you want,' I offered, jerking a thumb at the Transit. 'Do you know which way she would have gone?'

'Into the village probably. Are the pubs shut?'

I looked at my watch. Nearly 5.00 pm. 'Couple of hours ago.'

'We could check the off-licence, I suppose, though I didn't think she had any money.'

No, but she had some credit cards, I thought. 'Is it far?'

'Three miles.' Melanie turned to one of the other women and handed over Antiope. She also slipped her ball-bearings into her jeans pocket. 'Go and play, luvvie. Tricia, you come with me.'

Tricia turned out to be one of the plumper

members of the bodyguard, and she kept hold of her ball-bearings. From the look in her eyes, I wasn't going to make a smart remark about that either.

'What's this? A posse?'

Melanie looked me squarely in the face. 'We never travel alone with men.'

'Fair enough.' I unlocked the passenger door of the Transit for them, but I thought it best not to open it for them or offer them a hand up and in.

Tricia sat between Melanie and me, which made me change gear ever so carefully in case I brushed against her ample thigh, and Melanie shouted instructions around her. We found the village easily enough, though anyone travelling in the area in a Porsche had better not blink.

It had a pub, which looked decent enough, a small village green flanked by a post office, a small supermarket and, incongruously, a hairdresser's called Sylvia's; and while this could be the hairdressing capital of east Suffolk for all I knew, I bet Sylvia didn't get many takers from the peace camp.

There was also a bus shelter on the green, one of the old-style ones that have a bench seat. Lying across it like a stranded whale, if, that is, whales wear pink flying suits, was Carol. And she was singing. And she was drunk.

I parked the van alongside the bus stop,

and Carol swayed to her feet, thinking I was a bus. As she stood up, an empty wine bottle clattered off the bench and rolled down the pavement. The Transit being left-hand drive, I was nearest to her, so I did the gentlemanly thing. I locked the door, wound up the window and told Melanie and Tricia to go and get her.

They didn't need much encouragement. Almost instantaneously they were round the nearside and had the odious Carol backed up against the van trying to wave away their prodding, stabbing fingers. There was a lot of 'You unreliable bitch' and quite a few 'selfish' and 'dopey' cracks before Carol managed to fight back a bit and shout, 'All right, I'll get us some food.' She seemed to be getting quite violent, as I could feel the van sway from her leaning against it.

Much more of this and some nosey neighbour was bound to call local Plod, though from the look of the place, Camberwick Green probably had tougher policing.

I wound down the window and butted in.

'Hello, Carol, hop in. Door's open.'

'Who's he?' she asked Melanie, without looking at me.

'He's brought us some wheels, which is more than you did. Now get in the van.'

'All right, sister, all right.' With some difficulty, she slid open the side door and bundled herself in and spread herself across one of the triple seats. But only just.

Melanie closed the door and looked at me. 'Back to camp?'

'Why not? I've nothing better to do.' I smiled and her eyes smiled back enough to make me think the ice could just possibly melt there under the right circumstances. Tricia noticed it too, for she put herself between us again on the front seat and I heard the giveaway click-clack from her pocket. I can take a hint. There was a gleeful whoop from the back seats. Carol had found my Sainsbury's bag of booze faster than a sniffer dog could have.

'And which party are we all going to tonight?' she chanted, then burped loudly.

'Put it down, Carol, it's not yours,' said Melanie in a voice that could have cheered a hockey team on the playing fields of Roedean.

'Okay, okay. Naughty Carol. Carol's been a bad girl, so Carol has to be put in her place in front of the man.'

I clocked her in the driving mirror. She had stretched out, lying on her back, and was speaking in a little girly voice.

'Put a sock in it, you old cow, you've caused more than your usual quota of trouble today.'

I may be wrong, but I got the distinct impression that Melanie didn't think too highly of Carol. I decided to keep quiet and drive. Carol began to sing a very rude version of 'Pretty Flamingo', which made me think that the stories of graffiti in Ladies loos were all true.

Suddenly she sat up and put her podgy arms around the shoulders of both girls.

'Alrighty-tighty, Carol will make amends. Carol will do the shopping.'

'I don't think I want to know about this,' said Melanie, trying in vain to shake off Carol's arm.

'Now don't be such a straight, Miss Starchy Knickers. Carol will take care of everything. Lend me Melissa and the twins and we can still make the village shop before it shuts.'

Melanie looked over Tricia's bosom at me. 'Will that be okay?'

'Sure,' I said, wondering what I was agreeing to.

'Who's he? Pardon,' Carol burped again.

'I came to see you,' I said, turning down the farm, track to the camp.

'What does he want?' Carol was still addressing Melanie, ignoring me.

'He came to see you. He said so. There's no reason to talk as if he was dead.'

'But Melanie, sweetums–' the little-girl-lost voice again – 'you're always telling us never to talk to strange men.'

'Nobody can ever tell you anything, Carol.'

'But you try, Mother Hen, don't you.'

107

Carol put her hands on either side of Melanie's face and tried to twist it to receive a deep-throat kiss – her tongue was out and ready. We were nearing the camp, so I aimed for the ruts in the track and put my foot down.

It worked beautifully. Carol was bounced backwards into her seat and then sideways on the floor of the van, banging her head on the side in the process. There was a good deal of howling from her, and a few overripe adjectives, but she was better padded than the seats of the Transit. I hoped my tequila was intact.

We made the camp, and Melanie shot me a smile as she jumped out. Tricia backed her way out, never taking her eyes off me or letting her ball-bearings slip. Carol had more or less righted herself by the time I let her out of the side door.

Again Carol acted as if I wasn't there, swaying past me into the middle of the camp, where she put her hands on her hips and yelled: 'Melissa! Bring the kiddies, we're going shopping!'

That whole shopping trip was something I'd rather draw a veil over, not because it was mildly larcenous (okay, illegal) but because my street cred would be severely dented if the saga got out. However, it got me well in with the sisters of the peace camp.

Melissa turned out to be a small, jolly woman, maybe a teacher or a social worker, and the only woman I saw in the camp who wore a wedding ring. The twins were pretty young – I never was much good with babies – and were called Anastasia and Lucifer – yes, Lucifer. Poor sod, just because it was a he. That proved to me what I had always thought, that there's a very thin line between feminism and apartheid.

Still, Melissa was pleasant enough and said 'Hello' and asked if I minded driving them back to the village. Without waiting for an answer, she piled into the back – 'Aren't there any seat-belts for the twins?' – and Carol, determined to believe I did not exist, joined her, after loading something that I didn't see in through the rear doors.

It turned out to be a double pushchair for the twins, who were either two of the best behaved children in the world or had been drugged. Melissa unfolded it and strapped the twins in when we reached the village, and I parked in the pub car park, as instructed by Carol.

The village shop was a white weather-boarded building that had been badly converted into a supermarket. Badly, that is, if you were the owner, for I could see from the outside that the arrangement of the shelves provided loads of blind spots for shoplifters well out of sight of the cash till.

Not, of course, that such things were of interest to me. All I had to do was turn the van around and wait. Carol and Melissa pushed the twins across the road and then lifted the pushchair over the shop doorstep. I could see what went on through the two front windows, despite the '4p off Whiskas' stickers, and I have to admit I was impressed.

Carol distracted the white-coated male assistant, exercising commendable control by not kneeing him in the nuts as she no doubt would have liked to. He was probably the poor mug who owned the shop, and his wife was probably out back somewhere reheating his fish fingers for dinner. While he was talking to her, Melissa took the twins out of the pushchair and began to carry them around the store, one balanced on each hip, until she found somewhere to sit down. As the average age of the village population was probably about 70, it would be the sort of shop that had chairs littered all over it.

The next bit of business was Carol's, as she again distracted the old man in the white coat. By the time the witless victim had thought to go back to his cash desk, Melissa had juggled the twins sufficiently to pull her jumper up over her head and was offering a late lunch to Anastasia and Lucifer.

The shopkeeper, reasonably enough, went spare, and while I could easily imagine what he was saying to Melissa, I would have loved to have heard her side of the argument. She kept her cool and dished out more than her fair share of barefaced cheek, in more senses than one. He waved his arms about a fair bit and then disappeared to the back of the shop to be joined by, I presume, his wife for moral support.

While all this was going on, of course, Carol was flitting about the opposite side of the shop helping herself from the shelves and tossing things into the pushchair, which with the canopy zipped up was acting as an oversize shopping trolley.

To give her her due, she didn't overdo it. She allowed herself about three minutes, and then joined in the argument over Melissa while working the push-chair towards the door. The poor shopkeeper was so bemused that he actually opened it for her, and the pushchair came out first. Carol followed carrying one of the twins, and then Melissa with the other. The shopkeeper slammed the door behind them and quickly pulled down a blind with the word 'CLOSED' on it.

Carol was giggling insanely and Melissa was still trying to pull her jumper down over her unruly, but perfectly formed, breasts as they ran across the road to the van.

'No, like this. Hand over the glass, twice round, then slam.'

We had finished dinner and were sitting around the campfire. Dinner had consisted of tinned salmon, rye crispbreads and creamed cheese, Greek yoghurt with brown sugar and tinned mandarin oranges, but we weren't singing campfire songs. I was teaching them the fine art of drinking Tequila Slammers, one of the fastest ways of getting spifflicated known to man. Or in this case, wimmin.

'You're trying to get us tipsy,' Melissa observed. Clever girl.

'Sole purpose of exercise,' said I.

Melanie had joined us, having put Antiope to bed somewhere among the tents, and so had her minder, Tricia, though she wasn't slamming with us, rather contenting herself with a small carton of yoghurt drink and a straw.

The Tequila Slammer, which you probably won't find in the cocktail recipe books, was almost certainly invented by some loony Hooray in a flash cocktail bar somewhere as a means of using up cheap tequila. That sounds very 'snooty, as tequila isn't cheap in this country, but there's such a snob value on Tequila Gold these days that ordinary mescal juice simply won't do.

Basically, you take a good slug of tequila (ice cold if poss) and add a splash of lime-juice, then top up a five-ounce glass with champagne – or Sainsbury's Asti Spumante, whichever comes first to hand. Then you put your left hand over the glass, swirl it round two or three times in mid-air, slam the glass down as hard as you can on a hard surface and drink the lot in one. The theory is that the bubbles are evenly spread throughout the drink by the slam, but after one, who the hell cares?

We were drinking out of glass tumblers with British Rail logos on and generally chewing the fat and putting the world to rights.

'Thisisgood ... juice,' slurred Carol, who was over halfway to Smashed City Arizona already. 'Where did you say Dave was from?'

She was still talking about me rather than to me, so in a way I was glad I hadn't used any of my real names.

'Germany, wasn't it?' Melanie was warming to me. Or maybe it was the tequila.

'I've been out there for a year or so.' I set up another three Slammers, pouring the lime-juice and tequila together so that I could cut mine to about half the strength I was giving them. It's a good trick if you can do it.

'When did you get back?' asked Melanie.

'Yesterday. Came into Harwich on the ferry and called in the Uni on the off-chance.'

'Off-chance of meeting Carol?' The very thought made her pause in mid-slam.

'No, looking up an old friend called Jo.' I

glanced at Carol, but she was staring vacantly at the fire. 'And I ran into a guy called Alan who said Carol might know where she was.'

'Alan sent you?' Carol perked up. Obviously there still some solidarity among the '84 Four. It seemed a useful line to follow.

'Seems a straight type. He told me you'd be here. We did a little business.'

'Business?' A flicker of interest there as she downed her Slammer and rocked back on her haunches, but only at about Mark 5 on the Richter Scale.

'Just a little bit of trading.' I offered her more tequila, leaning across Melanie to do so. Either Melanie pushed some part of her anatomy against my leg or I was too close to the campfire.

'You dealing stuff for Alan? Pardon.' Carol broke wind at the other end this time. Maybe I was putting too much Asti in the Slammers.

'Just a little something from the groves of Lebanon, via downtown Dusseldorf, that is.'

'Got any left?'

'Some seed and grass. Wanna smoke?' What a question. Do fish swim?

I stretched up and strolled over to the Transit. Around me the camp was settling down for the night, bricks securing groundsheets, tent flaps tied tight, kerosene lamps hissing away their shadows. Ironically it looked more like a scene from after the nuclear holocaust instead of a plea to prevent one. I mean, can you imagine surviving with all these wimmin going round saying Told you so'?

I retrieved my stash from where I'd taped it under the steering column, and my cigarettes and green Rizla papers from the dashboard. It always seemed a waste to use up a couple of Gold Flake this way, but I always forget to buy cheaper cigarettes, and anyway, the corner tabs on the cardboard packets make excellent roaches.

I locked the Transit – you can take peace, harmony and sisterly love just so far – and threaded my way back through the tents to the fire Melanie had lit near the clapped-out bus without wheels. Tricia and Melissa had disappeared, probably in disgust.

Melanie had found some more wood, mostly bits of USAF fencing by the look of it. Carol hadn't moved, though the level of the tequila had.

'Who did you say you were looking for?' she asked suspiciously as I pulled up a weather-beaten bus seat.

'Jo. I heard she was a friend of yours.'

'Jo who?' She was clocking me from the corner of one bleary eye. I concentrated on rolling a very juicy joint.

'I don't think I ever knew her last name. She was at the Uni down the road, so I called in. Alan said you might know where she is.'

'Can't place her,' said Carol, but the piggy eyes never left the joint.

'Single strands?' I suggested, and Carol snapped yes so quickly I almost dropped the thing into the fire. Melanie said no, she'd toke on mine. In some countries that's virtually the same as going through a wedding service. In most countries it's preferable. I licked and rolled, then lit the joint and handed it to Carol. It was a humdinger. I rolled a much leaner version for Melanie and me to share.

'You do know a Jo, Carol,' said Melanie. 'You brought her up here once, or rather you got her to drive you here in that big flash Jaguar. Remember?' Melanie edged nearer and lowered her voice. 'Skinny, mousey blonde. Docile. Easy meat for the old bag.'

'Vaguely...' Carol drawled, then took a long draw, a good lung-and-a-half-full. 'Got any of these to spare?' she squeaked, trying to hold the smoke in.

'You're smoking my next six weeks' dole money,' I said, handing the second joint to Melanie.

'I'll buy some off you,' Carol exhaled, and her head disappeared in the cloud.

'With what, smart arse?' sneered Melanie. 'You were supposed to get us into town today to get our benefits, but you blew it.'

They argued some more while I poured out more Slammers, or rather Melanie argued and Carol grunted occasionally. She took the drink I offered without a word and downed it straight away, no longer even bothering to slam. After her fifth or sixth toke, she was down to the end of the joint, and a couple of the dried seeds exploded like miniature fireworks, making her jump and then starting her off giggling.

I placed the plastic bag of dope on top of the cigarette packet, in clear view, but made no move to roll her another joint. She was reluctant to let go of the roach at first, but then she hurled it into the fire and got unsteadily to her feet, saying, 'I know what.'

Her pink flying suit had two dirty orbs where her backside had imprinted itself on the ground, and I noticed for the first time that her trainers were at least size 9 (men's.) She seemed to be having trouble putting one in front of the other, but she did eventually make it to the steps of the disabled bus and fell inside. She was in there for a good five minutes, crashing around and swearing occasionally.

I made a facial question-mark at Melanie but she just shrugged and edged closer. Her rats-tail hair didn't seem so bad suddenly, and in the firelight she was quite pretty. I was going to have to ease up on the Slammers.

'Are you heading for London?' she asked,

handing me the dog-end of our joint.

'Yeah, but maybe not tonight.' I thought I'd better add a rider to that; it was easy to be male and misunderstood around here. 'I'll crash in the back of the van for a couple of hours before hitting the road; I'm too easy a target for the cops in that thing, and I'm over the limit.'

'Is it big enough for two?' she said, straight-faced.

'What about the sisterhood?' I said, indicating the surrounding tents.

'It's not that big, is it?' she giggled. Melanie had a nice giggle. I was going to have to ease up on the grass as well.

'I didn't mean that. I just got the impression that sex with a member of the opposite sex was frowned on round here.'

'Nah,' she drawled. 'We haven't castrated a man here for weeks – and anyway, Tricia's gone to bed.' She gave me that up-from-under look that only women can do without appearing cretinous. 'And it gets very cold around here at night.'

There was an extra loud crash from inside the bus, followed by a stream of invective calling into question the parentage of the Pope and his fondness for animals. Then Carol reappeared with what I first thought was cocaine down most of her right side.

She was clutching something in her right hand, something covered in white powder, as she weaved towards us and sat down heavily and out of breath. I poured her neat tequila, which she swilled greedily. 'How about these?' She held out her hand.

It was difficult to see what she was offering at first, but as I took them from her, I saw they were credit cards, an Access and a Visa, both made out in the name Mrs J A Scamp. I made sure I got some of the white powder on my fingertips and, not making a big deal of it, brought them up to my tongue. The powder was flour. Wholemeal. I handed them back, much to her surprise.

'You'd steal from another woman?' said Melanie indignantly. Men, it appeared, were fair game.

'A rich bitch who won't miss them,' Carol said dreamily. The effort of searching the bus had accelerated the effect of the alcohol and dope.

'I don't take payment by drastic plastic, I'm afraid.' I stuck two papers together and started to make another joint. Carol's face fell and I thought she might burst into tears.

'You can keep them ... in exchange,' she said slowly, holding them out like a magician would.

Melanie tuned in to the same image and whispered: 'Go on, pick a card, any card,' in a Tommy Cooper voice.

'Tell you what I'll do.' I finished the joint, lit it and handed it to Carol. It was another rich mixture. 'I'll see what value I can get on the street in town for these and I'll leave you this bag on the basis that if I can't dispose of them, I'll be back for it.'

'Sure, sure.' She sucked on the joint and put her head back. Now she could relax, she thought, if she was still capable of thinking. She had no intention of handing the joint back, but I didn't bother fixing another for Melanie and me. Instead, I just lit up a straight fag and shared it with her, Bogart style.

I moved the bag of grass over towards Carol, but kept hold of it.

'So you don't remember Jo, then?'

'Jo? Jo? Josephine...'

It was too late; she'd gone. Three minutes later, she was snoring gently. I palmed the credit cards into my jacket pocket so that Melanie didn't see me and rescued the still-smoking joint from Carol's fingers. I half-offered it, but Melanie shook her head, so I tossed it reluctantly onto the fire. I hate waste.

'We'd better get her inside,' I supposed.

'If we really must. Her pit's at the back of the bus.'

Melanie took her legs and I took the bows and we struggled up the steps, Carol's bum hitting most of them, which I reckoned Melanie was doing deliberately.

The interior of the bus was lit only by a

small torch made to look like an old lamp, the type you see in Westerns, and from what I could see I was glad there was no more light. The debris included empty wine bottles, food wrappers, part of a loaf of bread so hard the sparrows would bend their beaks, and a half-empty tin of baked beans with enough penicillin growing in it to supply most of Soho for a year.

Carol's 'pit' was the back seat of the bus piled high with old coats and a couple of threadbare blankets.

'We all had sleeping-bags when we came here,' said Melanie. 'The Christian CND sent them. Carol sold hers.'

'Heave.'

We dumped Carol face down and I leaned over to try and turn her. Never leave anybody in that condition face down. Not even a Carol.

As I leaned further, I felt a hand sliding up the inside of my left thigh. Christ, she's awake, I thought; then I realised it was coming from behind.

'What about Antiope?' I asked hopefully.

'She'll be asleep.' Melanie's voice had gone suddenly husky, as if the treble control on the stereo had failed.

'You'd better check,' I said without turning round. 'I'll make sure Carol's okay.'

'That cow will sleep through anything.' The grip on my thigh tightened.

'We don't want her choking on her own vomit, though, do we?'

'If you say so. See you in five minutes.'

As soon as she'd gone, I finished rolling Carol on to her side and threw a coat over her. Then I picked up the lamp-torch and held it above my head. I knew roughly what I was looking for, and I found it on the floor under a seat-frame from which the seat had been removed.

It was a brown paper bag of Jordan's Wholemeal Flour, about half full. Quite a bit had spilled over the floor already, so nobody would notice any more. Carol must have just dropped the bag when she fetched the credit cards.

I lowered the torch to floor level, just in case anyone was watching, and squeezed the bag gently. Yes, there was something in there, and I bet myself it would be Jo's emerald pendant. Wasn't it Chandler's *The Lady in The Lake* where Philip Marlowe finds the jewellery clue in a box of sugar? I put my hand in and found it. Well, I supposed it was an emerald under all that flour – either that or the millers were giving away some expensive free gifts these days.

I slipped it into my pocket and dusted off my hands and clothes. Carol hadn't stirred. Mission accomplished. Almost.

Melanie was waiting by the Transit holding two sleeping-bags, the sort that you can unzip and lay flat. I picked up my fags and the bag of grass from near the campfire and motioned her around to the driver's door. I wanted to keep the back door locked, and you couldn't do that from inside.

It turned out to be a wise precaution. During the night, the handle was tried at least twice.

CHAPTER SEVEN

I was back on the A12 heading south for the Smoke by 7.00 the next morning, well before the Front Line had stirred – all but Melanie, that is, who had been grumpily evicted from the Transit at 6.30. I was whistling a medley of Ellingtonia, keeping an eye out for a transport café for breakfast and feeling fairly pleased with myself. Not cocky enough not to watch my speed, though, nor to keep looking in the rear-view mirror. The Suffolk traffic cops were well-known to be a lot keener than their Essex brethren, and a van like this one coming away from a military establishment was a natural target at that time in the morning.

I found one of those plastic and formica Little Chefs that were replacing the old greasy spoon eateries and went straight into the Gents. There I dampened some paper towels and wiped the flour off the goodies I'd removed from Flaxperson. So that was an emerald.

It was smaller than I'd thought it would be for two-and-a-half grand's worth, but then what do I know? The pendant itself was heart-shaped, the emerald in the centre, and no bigger than my thumbnail. I presumed the metal was silver and the chain too. On the back of the heart was engraved 'JJ' in flowing script. A bit twee, I thought, for a prototype yuppie like Jo. Still, mine not to reason why.

I tucked into bacon and eggs and fried bread and pondered on the great philosophical issues of life such as why you never got fried black pudding for breakfast anymore. (It's now called *boudin* and is served with apple sauce and puréed carrots in *nouvelle cuisine* restaurants.) I had located the dreaded Carol easily enough, and reclaiming the pendant had been a piece of cake; well, a piece of more than cake, actually. I'd even found the missing credit cards.

All I had to do now was give them back.

Should have been easy. Shouldn't it?

I drove via Barking to call in on Duncan the Drunken before the traffic built up, but his garage was locked and that meant calling at the house. Unfortunately, Doreen was in.

'Hello, Fitzroy, chuck, how yer doin'?'

'Hi, Doreen. Where's Dunc?' I'd long since given up trying to get her not to call me that.

'Out – but on a job. When he's earning, I'm not complaining. Come in for a cuppa?'

I declined quickly. She might have offered me something to eat, as most Northern

125

women believe they have a mission in life to feed up any male who can still see his feet.

'I just called to return Duncan's van and pick up Armstrong – my cab.'

'You'll have to see the old man when he gets back. I told you, he's out earning. Be back about 5.00.'

'Oh no, not another wedding?'

Doreen smiled. It was all right for her, she didn't have to clean up the sodding confetti.

So I was stuck with the Transit for the rest of the day. If I parked that outside Stuart Street, it would really annoy Frank and Salome if they had friends round. So that's what I did.

Disappointingly, they were out when I got home, and so, it seemed, were Fenella and Lisabeth, but that Saturday was Lisabeth's jumble sale day. And of course there was no sign of Mr Goodson from the ground-floor flat; there never was at the weekend.

I checked behind the wall phone to see if any mail had been stuffed there for me but, as usual, there was nothing. Somebody had left me a note, though, through the cat flap in my flat door.

Springsteen circled my legs and howled a bad-tempered welcome as I opened the purple – yes, purple – envelope. On matching paper with a cartoon of Snoopy wearing a Harvard T-shirt, was written:

Dear Mr Angel

A nice lady called Mrs Boatman rang this afternoon (Friday) and said she was anxious to speak to you. Please ring her on Monday at Walthamstow DHSS office. Sorry, I forgot the number. Some secretary, eh?!!!

Love, Fenella.

I screwed the note into a ball and threw it for Springsteen to play with. He took a tentative bite and then started howling again, so I had to open a tin of Whiskas – turkey flavour, full price. (If I ever get any on special offer, I have to remove the price tags before he sees them.) Then it was a shower and a shave for me before planning Saturday Night Out.

As the house seemed empty, I got in four or five unlogged phone calls around the circuit of friends and acquaintances to see what was cooking. The menu was pretty basic as it turned out. Trippy was meeting somebody at a club down at Camden Lock, but he couldn't remember who or exactly where. I could guess why though. Bunny had got himself invited to a party down in Fulham at a house rented by four air hostesses who worked for Cathay Pacific. I didn't know whether that was good or not, and even Bunny admitted it was a leap in the dark, as his experience had not got above Sealink Duty Free Shop assistants in the past. There was no point in ringing Dod. In his book, Saturdays were for racing, betting and boozing – nothing else – and he rarely strayed beyond the local corner pub. I tried the Mimosa Club to see if anyone interesting was playing that evening, but got no reply. No surprises there, as Stubbly never bothered with the floating drinking trade on Saturday afternoons. After all, some of them might be football supporters.

I didn't call any female friends, for the idea was to take Jo out. Yet the options seemed limited. Maybe I should socialise more. I settled for the party in Fulham on Bunny's recommendation, arranging to meet him in a trendy pub in Covent Garden beforehand. Then I rang Jo, prepared to hang up if a man answered.

'Hello, Celia,' she said when she heard my voice. 'How did you make out?'

'Just fine. Mission accomplished. How would you like to reclaim your property? I take it I can't call round.'

'Quite right, Celia.'

'So you'll have to come to me. Can you sneak out tonight?'

'Maybe later.'

I told her I'd be in the Maple Leaf in Covent Garden until about 9.00, then down in Fulham, and I gave her the address of the party and told her to ask for Louise.

'Who's Louise?' she asked.

'Damned if I know,' I said truthfully, and she said Okay and See Ya and hung up.

I thought it a bit off that she'd never asked how I'd got her pendant back. I mean, I might have had to shove the split match heads under Carol's fingernails, or tie her to a tree and subject her to psychological warfare by, say, reading Hemingway aloud to her.

Knowing Carol, of course, it would have made more sense to ask if I'd come out of things in one piece – the piece in question being in the genitalia region. But Jo had done neither. There's gratitude for you.

Duncan had not returned Armstrong by 6.00, so I presumed it would be the next morning. I had no intention of taking the Transit up West – I'd had enough trouble round the launderette, which doubles as a common room for the junior branch of the Hackney National Front – so I left it parked outside the front door in exactly the spot where Frank and Salome usually plug in the nightlight for their VW Golf. (One day they'll knit it a pullover.)

Anyway, that meant I could have a decent drink and trust to luck not to have to need a lift back.

Whenever possible, I try and make a point of taking something special to a party. Now I know what you're thinking, but I mean to drink; something more appealing to women than the Carlsberg Special Brew brigade, something more interesting than Piesporter Michelsberg.

Stan at the local off-licence is my guide on this, though I think it's really his way of getting rid of old stock. That night, it was Kummel, a fresh packet of Gold Flake and about 40 quid (30 drinking money, ten in another pocket for emergency taxi home or suchlike), and, dressed in my Who Bears Wins sweatshirt and long brown leather jacket, I was ready to roll. I wrapped Jo's pendant in some soft toilet paper and lodged it in the jacket's inside pocket. And I picked up a pack of contraceptives. I mean, it's not that I'm scared by the Government's advertising campaign on safe sex, I'm just very socially responsible.

I hopped on a bus to King's Cross and then took a tube round to Leicester Square, missing out Covent Garden station as the lifts were out of action again. (There are prizes for anyone who can remember them working.)

The streets were full of theatregoers, tourists and buskers and ticket touts looking for the tourist theatregoer. I dropped some change to a lone mandolin player doing a slow-tempo 'Sweet Georgia Brown', partly because he was good and partly because he might do the same for me someday. Then I called in at the Vecchio Reccione near String-fellows for a glass of Valpolicella and a bread stick. 'The Vetch' is a really good restaurant; so good, I can't afford to eat there, but I have played there on occasions and most of the staff know me well enough to stop for a drink and a chat. Their trademark is anarchy. The waiters don't have menus, they come and shout at you, and if you're sitting 'upstairs' on the ground floor, as opposed to the much more plebby basement, then they turn the lights off every 20 minutes or so and all the diners have to dance by candlelight for two minutes whether they want to or not.

It was about 8.30 when I got to the Maple Leaf, London's only Canadian pub. Thank God. When it first opened, it sold Molson Ale on draught, which is not a bad drink at all. Not an ale, but not bad. Nowadays it sells bottled lager, which the trendies drink from the bottle because it's what they think Canadians do, and Watneys bitter at a leg-and-an-arm a pint. You can tell it's a Canadian pub, because it has a lot of pine. Otherwise its only distinguishing feature is that the staff chalk up the latest Canadian baseball and ice hockey scores on a black-board, genuinely believing that people are interested.

Bunny was already there, sitting with a couple of young girls straight out of what the advertising men call the Sharon and Mandy market, and a tall, thin, angular guy with close-cropped blond hair.

'Just in time,' said Bunny. 'Two Pils and two halves of Snakebite. This is Dosh and Freddie.' He pointed to the girls. 'And this is Chase. Meet Angel.'

'Angel? I wouldn't mind him sitting on top of my Christmas tree,' said either Dosh or Freddie. I made a note to find out which. If they were on Snakebite, I'd better do it quickly.

I got the drinks in and discovered that Dosh and Freddie were flat-sharing in Willesden and were both typists up from darkest Bedfordshire a mere three months before in search of bright lights, word-processor experience and more than six grand a year. God knows where Bunny had found them.

Chase turned out to be a tuba player, of all things, though I would have put him down as backing vocals for the Communards on appearances alone. While it's always good to know the odd tuba player (and let's face it, most of them are), Chase unfortunately was a fanatic, believing that there had been no good jazz since the King Oliver band. Because I said I liked the immortal Bix Biederbecke, he obviously thought I was *avant garde* and beyond redemption. Then I mentioned that I had a Lawson Buford tuba solo from 1927 somewhere in my record collection and I was back in favour. Which was a bad move, as I hate jazz bores and usually much prefer the company of bored typists from Willesden.

By 9.30 there was no sign of Jo, so I suggested we headed off to Fulham. Dosh and Freddie didn't take much persuading, but Chase thankfully declined, saying that parties didn't like him.

Bunny drove an old Vauxhall, probably older than himself, because it had a bench front seat and column change and gear levers got in the way. He made sure that Dosh – or Freddie – sat next to him, so I ended up with Freddie – or Dosh – in the back seat, and she was getting very friendly by the time we got to Knightsbridge.

The party was in a big house on Fulham Palace Road, and in full swing when we got there. In other words, the lights were off in the living-room except for the strobes around the disco where a lonely DJ was pumping out Frankie Goes to Hollywood, and all the guests at the party were in the kitchen cluttering up the fake-oak work-surfaces and obscuring the Neff oven.

Over by the spice rack, a George Michael lookalike was arguing with a Jimmy Sommerville doppelganger. They'd probably end up the best of friends. By the coffee machine, a real Medallion Man was boring two women with the 'Lucky Harry' joke. It wasn't that they were prudish; I could tell they'd heard it before. A pair of nattily suited yuppie executives, complete with red-and-black braces, were sharing a bottle of lime-flavoured Perrier by the sink and discussing futures in the zinc market in between swapping Porsche stories. All in all, standard fare.

Bunny introduced me to a big redhead (the Fergie look) wearing a flimsy black party frock slit up both sides to reveal large expanses of lace-patterned black tights. You know, the sort that make thick calves look even thicker and are worn only by women with thick calves. Her name was Louise, she said, as she grabbed me and planted a long kiss, tongue first.

'They told me trumpet-players could kiss,' she said, breaking free.

'Oh, and you thought they meant on the mouth?' I said innocently.

Louise turned on her three-inch heels and clicked away. So much for our hostess.

'I can see why you don't get invited to many parties,' said Bunny.

'But I'll survive as long as I can sponge off urbane socialites like you, Bunny.'

He ripped a couple of ring-pulls and offered me a lukewarm Fosters.

'But I always voted Conservative.'

'Let's find Dosh and Freddie. I fancy some intellectual stimulation.'

Bunny raised no more than an eyebrow, and we shouldered our way through to the hall where Dosh and Freddie were discovering that they could really get to like Kummel.

Just after 11.00, more people began to arrive as the pubs chucked out, and so Dosh (or maybe it was Freddie) and I moved upstairs, where we'd found another front room that had been stripped of furniture and somebody had run a pair of extra speakers off the disco in the lounge. Again, the light level was subterranean, but there were no curtains, so a fair amount of yellow light came in from the streetlamps outside.

Dosh – I was pretty sure it was Dosh – and I danced some, and she finished off the Kummel, which meant we then had to sit down for a while near the window, where some scatter cushions had been laid. She told me how much more exciting Willesden was than rural Bedfordshire, despite the once-a-year trips to Milton Keynes. I also got to hear how she intended to jack in her job at the insurance brokers just as soon as they'd taught her how to use the word-processor, and go and work somewhere interesting like in an ad agency or for a travel agent. She confirmed my suspicions that the majority of office computers in London contain nothing more vital than the personal

135

CVs of thousands of job-hunting junior staff. Maybe Bunny could learn to moonlight on a mainframe somewhere and tap into a whole new reference work of nubile young ladies. I'll put it to him one of these days.

I was standing up, offering to go downstairs to get more drinks, and glancing out of the window when I saw Jo.

She arrived in a big BMW of the type the East End villains drive now that all the old Jags have been bought up by the TV stations to make cops and robbers series. And she got out of the passenger side, which meant somebody else was driving. (That was good thinking, I thought. Obviously I hadn't had enough to drink.)

Sure enough, Jo leaned over to the driver's window and said something to someone before she ran up the steps to the house.

'Lemme get us some drinks,' I said to Dosh.

'Okay,' she smiled. 'Make mine a white swine.'

I found Jo in the hall trying to get through the serum of people to the kitchen. What is it about kitchens at parties that brings out the homing pigeon in everybody? She'd been waylaid within ten feet of the front door, which didn't surprise me, by a chinless wonder in a baggy suit and powder blue trainers. (Nobody wears trainers with a suit any more.) He was saying, would you believe, 'And where have you been all my life?'

'She wasn't born for most of it,' I interrupted, putting an arm round her and drawing her away.

Jo slipped an arm around my waist as we stood at the foot of the stairs.

'You've got it?'

I produced the emerald pendant wrapped in the toilet paper. She covered it with her hand immediately as if she was trying to hide it from prying eyes. Actually, nobody gave us a second look, as they must have presumed I was trying to get her upstairs to get inside her knickers.

She crammed it, tissue and all, into the left pocket of her fur coat, which I hoped was either fake or farmed, without looking at it. Then she delved into an inside pocket and produced a brown paper bag, the sort you get at off-licences.

'This is for you. It's as much as I could get so quickly. I thought it would take you longer.' She looked me in the eyes, not smiling.

'One quick raid into enemy territory was all it took. I'd like to say it was nothing, but I'd be lying.'

I peeked in the bag. There was a half-bottle of vodka – 'For the party,' Jo whispered – and a bundle of £20 notes wrapped with an elastic band.

'There's two hundred there. It was all I could get out of the hole-in-the-wall this evening. I owe you another 50, as we agreed.'

'I owe you something too,' I said, mentally kicking myself.

'What?' Her eyes opened just that little bit too wide.

'Your credit cards. I retrieved them too, but I've left them in my flat.'

'You're not holding out deliberately, are you? Trying to up the price?' She took a step backwards, which was about as far as she could go in that hallway. Some more guests arrived and pushed by me, pushing me on to her.

'Hey, now look...' I started.

'I'm sorry,' she said, looking over my shoulder at the open front door. 'I didn't mean it the way it sounded. I'll get the money to you. Don't worry about the cards, I'll say I lost them or got mugged. Just get rid of them. I'll send you the cash.'

She pulled the fur around her. 'I must go.'

'Hey, it's no hassle. I can drop the cards round anytime.'

'No.' Emphatic. 'Don't do that. Don't ring either. I'll send you your money. Just stay clear.' She touched me on the arm. 'Please.'

Then she was gone, just like that, pulling the door closed.

I moved into the front room, where the disco had moved on to heavier metal (New

Model Army, I think – a band to watch, despite their fans), but still nobody was dancing. From the front window, I saw Jo climb into the BMW and, as the interior light went on, I could make out the shape of the man driving. But only the shape. Still, what the hell business was it of mine?

I took the wad of twenties out of the bag and stuffed them into the back pocket of my jeans. I decided to take the vodka up to Dosh and tell her it was white wine.

I screwed up the brown bag and flipped it behind one of the disco's speakers. Jo must have at least four bankers' cards to get £200 out of the hole-in-the-wall bank machines, I figured, as £50 is usually the limit. Curious. And even more curious – they don't usually dispense £20 notes.

Still, mine not to reason why. It would pay the rent and keep the nice Mr Nassim Nassim off my back for another month. I pushed by a couple of drunks who had just appeared bearing the same bottle of Hirondelle they'd been using to get into parties all year and made my way upstairs.

I took it all philosophically. Never let women get you down. Well, not mentally. And anyway, Willesden isn't such a bad place to wake up in, even with a hangover.

CHAPTER EIGHT

I found Bunny in the girls' kitchen the next morning trying to find something to eat that wasn't raw carrot, muesli or Ryvita, and something to drink other than herbal tea.

'Sleep well?' he said, straight-faced.

'Fine. I think.' My mouth felt as if I'd swallowed a cheese-grater, and my scalp had suddenly acquired radioactive dandruff. 'How's Freddie?'

'How do I know? You slept with her.'

Oh Christ. That'll teach me to look in future. I decided to bluff it out.

'No, I was with Dosh.'

'Yeah, until we got in the car to come here.' He sniffed at a half-empty carton of goat's milk yoghurt. There appeared to be nothing else in the small fridge. 'Where did you get that bottle of tequila?'

'It was vodka, wasn't it?'

'No, the one after the vodka. You spent half an hour looking for lemons and salt.'

Oh no.

I went to the sink and turned the cold tap on for a long drink to combat the dehydration. With my head turned sideways, I could see out of the window and through the house to Willesden Sports Centre, where a Sunday league football team was working out. Just watching them made me feel ill.

'Do you wanna get out of here?' I asked, straightening up gently.

'Might as well, there's nothing to eat.'

'They must be on the F-Plan diet.'

'What's that?'

'You get fuck-all to eat.'

Bunny curled a lip. 'Oh, very quick. Not funny, but very quick. Come on, the pubs'll be open in five minutes.'

Oh, you bastard, Bunny.

Funnily enough, I felt better after a couple of pints at a pub in Maida Vale; you know, the trendy one among *Guardian* readers that has the really stupid long name and brews its own beer in the cellar. Not that the hair of the dog remedy actually works; it just makes you forget how bad you feel for a while.

I lunched on a cheese roll and a packet of crisps while Bunny – no day is wasted – chatted up the sulking wife or girlfriend of one of the lunchtime real ale bores who was drinking his way round the hand-pumps with a group of mates. At one point, I saw Bunny write something, probably her phone number, on a drip mat and slip it into the back pocket of his jeans. Like a flash, I thought to check my pockets.

All my cash was accounted for and Jo's ten crispy twenties were in place. My, but they're honest in Willesden, and the rent would get paid in Hackney.

I got Bunny out of the pub just before chucking-out time, and with a bit of persuasion he agreed to take me as far as Hackney, dropping me off at the end of Stuart Street. The first thing I noticed was that the Transit had gone and Armstrong was back in his place of honour outside No 9.

I did a quick walk-round check. Yes, there were still four wheels (well, you never know these days) and, just as I'd thought, the interior was littered with sodding confetti. I patted Armstrong's stubbly radiator and promised him a good clean-out. A pensioner walking his dog on the other side of the street quickened his pace, obviously not wanting to be there when the men in white coats came for me. Silly old buffer. I'll bet he talks to his dog.

Which made me think of Springsteen and the fact that he hadn't been fed for nearly 24 hours. He'd have my leg off.

But wonders (Rule of Life No 3) never cease. Outside my flat, sitting on the stairs, legs curled and making soft purring noises, was Fenella.

Next to her, his face stuck into a plate of what looked like raw mince, was Springsteen. I could see from the four small puncture marks on Fenella's wrist that she had tried to stroke him during lunch. Silly girl. He's an ungrateful bastard at the best of times, but biting the hand that feeds you *while* it's feeding you is a bit out of order.

'Hello, Fenella,' I said, because she wouldn't have spoken if I hadn't. 'Has he conned you as well?' She smiled a really nice smile. 'Don't tell me, let me guess: the scratching at the door, the piteous crying, the sucked-in, ever-so-thin ribs...'

She nodded and sighed.

'Yeah. Taught him everything I know.'

That brought a spot of colour to her cheeks when she'd worked it out.

'I couldn't stand it any more – hearing him howl, I mean. But it was Lisabeth who got the mince for him. I had to feed him, though; she's not a cat person.'

'Hey, there's nothing nasty in there, is there? I mean, you're not missing a light bulb or anything, are you?'

'Don't be awful, Angel, she's just trying to butter you up.'

'Coming from anyone else, Fenella, that would be rude, but I know you're a well-brought-up young...' The penny dropped. 'Your parents are coming, aren't they, and she wants to move in with me.'

'And you'd forgotten. She said you would.'

Fenella can be really prissy sometimes.

'When are you expecting them?'

143

'Tonight, about 6.00. I'm cooking vegetable curry for them.'

I was sure they could hardly wait; but then to be fair to Fenella, she was the only woman under 50 I knew in London who made her own damson jam. Most women in London work on the theory that if you can't microwave it, only the ethnic minorities can cook it.

'And when does Lisabeth want to move into the annexe? Not that I mean to make her sound like some latter-day Anne Frank, of course.'

'She's more or less packed.'

Springsteen finished the mince and inspected his whiskers for any he'd missed. Fenella retrieved her plate, keeping an eye out for the fastest claw in the East End.

'Well, send her up,' I said, putting my key in the flat door. Springsteen shot between my legs through the catflap without another look at Fenella. Typical male: eats and runs.

'I'd better give her a hand or she'll sulk. You wouldn't have thought she had so much stuff.' Fenella started down the stairs. 'Who was Anne Frank, Angel?'

'Before your time, luv. And don't ask Lisabeth.'

She might know.

By the time the aged parents had arrived, Lisabeth was ensconced in my bedroom, the sleeping-bag (which has seen me through three continents, two sit-ins, an eviction and a New Year's Eve in Trafalgar Square, and which I called Hemingway) in place on the sofa. Springsteen tested it for comfort, then hid under the low coffee table, partly because it's the only table I have and partly because it's the ideal place to ambush somebody coming out of the bedroom with no shoes on.

I went downstairs to help the Binkworthys in with their bags, and also to get a look at them as I was mildly curious, not to mention nosey.

Mr Binkworthy was a tall, dapperly-dressed bloke who had parked his redundancy-money Ford Sierra behind Armstrong. He looked at it suspiciously, and almost as if contemplating a sly kick at one of the wheels, as he unloaded the food parcels the diminutive and cheery Mrs Binkworthy thought Fenella needed. I said it was mine.

'So you're a musher, are you?' he said, showing off.

'Sort of. Yes, I own my own cab, but the real mushers would have me if I took a fare.'

He let me take a box of groceries (Sainsbury's of course) while he unloaded a couple of suitcases from the boot. I told him to lock the car.

'But we're coming back. There's more stuff on the back seat.'

'Lock it or lose it.' He took my advice, and I could see him thinking that maybe this wasn't the best sort of area for his only daughter.

'Don't worry,' I soothed. 'It's mostly kids after cassettes or petty cash in the glove compartment.'

He didn't seem convinced, so I didn't tell him that I wouldn't give odds on his wheels being there in the morning.

'So you're a neighbour of Fenella's?' he huffed as he strained up the stairs.

'Yup, next flat up. I've been here for nearly a year now.'

He paused outside Fenella's open door. From inside, there came the clink of crockery and Mrs Binkworthy's high-pitched voice feigning joviality.

'I was very worried when Fenella came to live in London, I don't mind telling you,' he confided; so, as a totally unconcerned complete stranger, I tut-tutted sympathetically. 'She's very young for her age, you know.' Well, so was I. 'And her mother and I have always worried about her.'

My God, they suspected!

'She's been so sheltered from men, you know. All her life. Convent school, then secretarial college. We felt sure she'd be preyed on when she came to the big city.' He smiled thinly and shrugged his shoulders. 'Still, she appears to be looking after herself.

Tell me honestly – you seem to be a friend – does she have any trouble with boyfriends?'

I looked him straight in the eye. 'No, Mr Binkworthy, I can truthfully put your mind at ease on that score.'

The things I do for people.

Which reminded me, I had some credit cards to return. I wasn't put off by the fact that Jo had told me not to call or see her. She'd obviously been confused and had things on her mind. Anyway, she owed me 50 quid.

And as there was a serious possibility of being invited in for tea and vegetable curry, I thought it wise to make myself scarce. It wasn't that I minded Fenella, and I could have had fun doing a wind-up on her parents. No, the reason I dare not go would be the prospect of facing Lisabeth's jealousy for the rest of the week. As it was, she pumped me about every move the Binkworthys had made since their arrival, before settling down with a mug of Bovril and a packet of salt 'n' vinegar to watch American football on the box. I hadn't realised she was a fan, but it explained how she walked the way she did.

While she was deciding whether to support the Denver Broncos or the Pittsburgh Pederasts (whatever), I sneaked into the bedroom and nearly had a heart attack to find a three-foot Paddington Bear propped up on the pillow. How had she got that in without me seeing? But I wasn't going to ask.

I took down from the bookshelf above the bed a hardback edition of Hugh Brogan's *History of the United States*. I usually keep it between the Tolkiens and the MacDonalds (John or Philip, not Ross). It's actually quite a good book, and I'd had a few qualms about turning it over to Lenny the Lathe, who specialises in converting books more than an inch thick into fireproof, combination-lock safes. But he'd owed me a favour for a little job I'd done him and I'd needed somewhere to stash my passport, emergency cash and one or two other goodies. After all, there are 11 million people in the Naked City and only some of them are honest.

I removed Jo's credit cards from the book-safe and returned it carefully, just in case Lisabeth got nosey. I had few worries that she would suddenly take an interest in American history, but she might notice something out of place, and the combination lock looked much more sophisticated than it actually was.

Before leaving, I gave a spare key to Lisabeth and an envelope with Jo's two hundred quid for her to give to Mr Nassim. (Being a Muslim, he didn't mind collecting rent on a Sunday.)

'Oh God, is it rent day again?' Lisabeth moaned. 'Okay, I'll see the thief of Baghdad for you. In fact, it might be better if I head him off before he gets to our place. The Binkworthys will have a fit if they see old Gunga Din Rachman. Are you going to be late?'

I paused mid-way through zipping up my black, waterproof blouson, which advertised (discreetly) Coors Lite. Lousy beer, but a good jacket with more than a few memories of a young lady from Boulder, Colorado, attached to it.

'Shouldn't think so. Why?'

'I was going to have an early night, but I won't bother if you're going to come in pissed and play your Little Feat LPs around midnight.'

'Don't worry, fair maiden, I shall return before the witching hour,' I said, edging towards the door. 'Oh, and don't worry about the snoring.'

'Snoring?'

'Yes. I've got earplugs, so don't worry about it.'

I was out of the flat before she could turn her head, and as I passed Springsteen on the stairs, I said: 'You're on your own, kid.'

Armstrong zipped through the City with more than usual aplomb, which made me think that Duncan the Drunken had given

149

him a tuning. He could never see an engine without laying a spanner on it. Not that there was much traffic about on a Sunday evening, and I was able to park right outside Sedgeley House.

The street door was locked, so I pressed the button numbered 11 on the squawk box built into the porch. There was no name tag in the oblong strip next to the button, but that wasn't unusual. The only people left in London who put their name on their doorbells these days were called Monica or Helga, and there was rarely a surname.

There was no answer. I could have saved some diesel and phoned. Then the old porter I'd seen on my first visit shambled across the hallway, teapot with no lid in one hand and a bottle of milk in the other.

I tapped on the armour-plated glass, but he couldn't or wouldn't hear me, so I pressed the button marked 'Reception' and the old buffer jumped vertically like a Harrier with wind.

He came to the door carefully, mouthing 'Whaddya-want?' I couldn't blame him; only a few days before, an eminent surgeon had been badly mugged in the entrance to his Harley Street office in the middle of the afternoon. Not only were the streets no longer safe, the lobbies were becoming risky too.

The old man put a deadlock on the door

before opening it.

'Flat 11,' I said. The bell doesn't seem to be working.'

'Bell's working, but there ain't nobody in, and I don't know when anybody'll be back. Is there a message?'

'No...' Over his shoulder, I could see the light above the lift doors flick on No 4. Top floor. Flat 11? 'Er... Has Mrs Scamp gone out?'

'Yes, this afternoon. Any message?'

The light showed the lift coming down.

'And Mr Scamp?'

'Oh, he's away a lot. Haven't seen him for months.'

'Okay, thanks.'

I turned away and took a step back into the twilight. The lift stopped in the lobby and the doors opened. I didn't know the man who stepped out and looked straight at the door, which the old buffer porter had managed to close. I think they spoke to each other, but I didn't get a good look until I was sitting in Armstrong with the engine running.

I could see them clearly in the light of the foyer, but they couldn't see me cloaked in the anonymity of Armstrong – and what more anonymous than a black London cab?

No, I'd definitely not seen the man coming out of the lift before. But he was a big man, and for some reason I had an unhealthy picture of him being more than able to do something unspeakable to Tonka toys.

Sunday night was usually jam session night at the Mimosa Club for assorted trad jazzmen who weren't in regular bands or who couldn't get a gig in one of the big suburban pubs. It was still early, so I didn't expect many customers, but I did expect more than one – me.

There was a Django Reinhardt tape playing – I know, because I recorded it and sold it to Stubbly – and Ken the barman was sitting on a bar stool reading the *News of the World*.

'Business booming, I see,' I said.

Ken didn't look up until he'd finished the story he was reading, and only then when his lips had finally stopped moving.

'It's gonna be a wasted evening. I told him it would be. I suppose you want a drink?' He moved his bum and made his way round the bar.

'Half a lager.'

'Him again,' snorted Ken.

'Eh?'

'Arthur Lager, regular customer.'

'And an old one.'

'The old ones are the best.'

'That's what we toy boys always say.'

Ken curled a lip in a half-snarl and slopped the beer over to me. From the foam on it, I guessed it was the first out of the keg that evening.

'Be a pound.'

'No staff discount?'

'No staff. Not tonight; the session's cancelled.'

'Cancelled? What about all those young talents who are drawn here every Sunday? Where will they go?'

'There's always the night shelter at Tottenham Court Road. I suppose I'd better put up the notice.'

Ken reached down under the bar and produced a homemade sign. It was a sheet of white paper stuck on to cardboard on which was typed: 'LIVE MUSIC CANCELLED UNTIL FURTHER NOTICE PENDING LICENCE RENEWAL APPLICATION – W. STUBBLY (PROP.)'

'So no gig on Tuesday?'

'Was there one booked? I never notice these days.'

'Another new band, so I'd heard. Style leaders in electronic reggae called Warmharbour Coldharbour, with a lead singer called Effra.' Ken looked totally underwhelmed.

'After Effra Road, Brixton.'

Ken lost interest completely. For the moment, he contented himself with pinning the notice to the inner door of the club and taking great delight in reading it to two young black guys who had arrived carrying saxophone cases. They decided not to stay, which pleased Ken no end.

'Stubbly could be missing out badly,' I said. 'One of those guys could have been the next Courtney Pine.'

'Who's he?'

'Just about the best British sax player since Tubby Hayes.'

I knew what was coming.

'Who? I thought your mate Rabbit was the bee's knees. By the way, did he get off with that drummer Richard last week?'

Ken picks up street talk like Sunday newspaper diarists pick up gossip, late and usually third-hand. 'Richard,' for the female of the species, derives from Richard the Third rhyming with 'bird,' but was now well past its sell-by date. The current term was 'Shaz,' meaning any female over 18 who went to Spain on holiday with boyfriend 'Chaz.' It came from green windscreen visors with 'Sharon & Charles' printed on, the 'Charles' always on the driver's side. And yes, it is sexist.

'No, I don't think he ever did score with that one. You reckon we should ring the day on the calendar?'

Ken snorted. It could have been a laugh, it could have been asthma.

'How about you? Did the bouncing handbag find you?'

'Eh?' Ken is one of the few people who can stun me into being ungrammatical. And incoherent.

'The two dykes who were in here that same night. One of 'em came back to see Stubbly and asked after you.'

'Which one?'

'The one that didn't look like Dumbo.'

'So she saw Stubbly, did she?' And got my address.

'Yeah, and she's been in a few times since. Didn't think you were into dykes, though.'

'She's no dyke, Kenny, and don't bother to ask how I know. And what do you mean – she's been in since?'

'Oh, just to chat with Stubbly. She was in last night, late on. I was just leaving. So she's straight, is she?'

I finished my beer.

'Just take my word for it, Kenny, and don't lose sleep over it. Would that be around tennish?' It was worth a try.

'Naw, much later. Oneish. Most everybody had gone. Everybody had gone, come to think of it, 'cos Stubbly shut the disco off at midnight.'

'Was she alone?'

'No, she came in with Nevil, the new bouncer. Sorry, doorman.'

'A big feller?'

'Brick shithouse proportions, squire. You don't want to dabble with the blonde Richard while she walks in Nevil's shade.' He cracked his face into what would be a sneer if it was more human.

'Or maybe you should mind your own business.' I started to leave. 'Oh, Kenny.'

'Yeah, what?'

'Why do you call them bouncing handbags?'

'Cos they looked like a couple of lesbians.'

'Yeah, I got that far. Why are their handbags supposed to bounce, though?'

'Because of the big rubber dildos they carry with them.'

Oh yes, of course. How logical. And I had to ask, didn't I.

CHAPTER NINE

For a couple of days, I got on with life's rich pageant without thinking any more of Jo or her bloody credit cards. Why didn't I just post them to her? I've asked myself since a hundred times.

Life with Lisabeth in the flat, which I had expected to be anything but a rich pageant, turned out to be not half bad. This was mainly due to the fact that when she was in residence, I contrived to be out. Still, she kept the place tidier than it had been for months, and she didn't mistreat Springsteen, or if she did, he didn't complain about it. And usually he is one of the biggest moaners around when I have guests.

Monday and Tuesday I had some regular work lined up, moving fire-damaged gin from a couple of pubs in Canning Town all the way across town to a warehouse in Hounslow.

Dod had got me the job and we were using his van, so everything was okay by me. If it had been anyone else, then, yes, even I would have said, 'How can you have fire-damaged gin?' But as it was Dod, I took my 50 quid and free ploughman's lunches (not that Canning Town's seen a ploughman since Shakespeare packed 'em in over at the Globe in Southwark) and we humped boxes and sat in traffic jams and set the world to rights. Well, if not the world, we at least sorted out Tottenham's back four.

Tuesday evening and there was rumour of a gig in a pub in Islington, with the added plus that – so the rumour went – good old loony left Islington Council were subsidising it. In other words, any immigrant, disabled, single-parent, unemployed, lesbian trombonist could get a grant for turning up. No, that's not fair. I'm sure the Council do a lot of good work, and it shouldn't fall to me to propagate the views of the monopolistic, right-wing press. There. Everybody happy now? The pub seemed to be the only building left standing (a good motto for the local council?) on that side of Copenhagen Street. It had been bought by a Northern brewery who couldn't believe that they could get over a pound a pint for their best bitter despite what they'd heard about Londoners. Still, they were making an effort, putting on cheap food and jazz bands, and so far the locals from the high rise flats across the road seemed to be accepting them. Well, at least the pub still had all its windows.

The band was a right dog's breakfast, with no bass player, an over-enthusiastic banjoist and a jealous pianist who thought he was being diddled out of his fair share of solos. Needless to say, the band was run on cooperative lines, with no-one in particular leading. By the time I got a look-in, two other trumpeters had pitched for a spot on the makeshift stage, so four of us did a loud, but enthusiastic version of 'Tiger Rag', which pleased the punters. Thank God they weren't jazz fans.

I'd seen Bunny arrive, take one look around the pub and decide against it. He stuffed his sax case under a table and ordered a pint at the bar, moving ever so casually towards two women sitting by themselves on high stools. They'd gone to the loo together by the time I joined Bunny. Maybe he was losing his touch.

'Not your scene?' I asked.

'I'm a Keep Music Live man; you know that. This is dead zone material.'

'I have to agree. Still, the ale's not bad, and I thought there might be a chance of a blow.'

'So did I,' said Bunny, looking towards the Ladies and wondering if there could be another exit he couldn't see. 'What's going down at the Mimosa?'

'Not a lot, as far as I know. Why?'

'Old Stubbly seems determined to put himself out of business. No music and the bar's only open for the minimum time he can get away with. Even the afternoon dipsomaniacs are deserting him now Kenny's gone.'

Behind me, the band, now augmented by two extra trombonists, broke into 'Beale Street Blues', and a tall, anorexic blonde who thought she knew the words volunteered to sing. It could have been that, I suppose, that made the hairs on the back of my neck feel like they were giving off static.

'Ken the barman? But I saw him Sunday evening.'

Bunny buried his face in his beer and I only just caught what he said over the noise from the band.

'Well, it must have been after that he had his accident.'

'Accident?' Why did I have to ask?

'Walking into his car door like that; really strange. Broke his nose, split his lip and blacked his eye. Couldn't go to work looking like that, could he?'

'Ken hasn't got a car.'

'I know. That's the really strange thing about it. But I wouldn't go there asking after him if I were you.'

I definitely wasn't going to ask this one. The anorexic blonde was on her fifth chorus. I never knew there were so many E-flats in it.

'Rod Stewart could have a voice like that if he smoked more,' I said, for the sake of something to say.

Bunny had finished his beer and the two

ladies were still in the Ladies, or had escaped without him seeing how. Either way, he was getting itchy feet.

'Okay, Bunny, do tell me why I shouldn't ask after Ken.'

'Because somebody was asking Kenny about you when he had his accident.'

'Asking what about me?'

'Who you is, where you're at.'

'Cut the street crap. Who and why?'

'Well, the why's not known. Or at least Kenny had no idea why anyone should think he was an oppo of yours, and he could tell them virtually zilch. He doesn't know your gaff or anything, does he?'

'So who was asking?'

'Stubbly's new doorman, it seems. A big guy called Nevil. Wears suits a lot, doesn't use words when he talks.'

Bunny grinned impishly. I hate him sometimes.

'So this Nevil asks Ken about me and then Ken runs into a car door, eh? Is that it?'

'More or less; but I've a feeling Nevil was holding the car door at the time.'

I refused to let this worry me. And, anyway, I only cruised up and down outside the house twice just to make sure there was no-one lying in wait.

Wednesday was an Even Rudergrams day for me, and that was usually good for a laugh.

Even Rudergrams was a new small company set up with the help of various Government enterprise grants (God Bless Our Lady of Downing Street), which specialised in an over-the-top kissogram service. All in the worst possible taste. Rudergrams went where even regular kissogram companies failed to boldly go. They had hit on the idea of advertising (discreetly) in things like the *Financial Times* and the *Economist*. This brought them a very high class of customer who didn't mind paying over the odds for something that little bit naughtier.

I was, of course, simply their innocent driver; well, most Wednesdays anyway. I had been trying to negotiate the Friday lunchtime run, which was the most lucrative, office-party wise, as ER was always on the lookout for reliable drivers who could not only deliver their people but hang around and pick them up. Inevitably they would be in an arrestable state of undress.

Today I had three of them in the back of Armstrong, the ideal vehicle for such a job, as a cab was unlikely to get moved along or clamped at a delicate, or indelicate, moment.

Clara and Rebecca had previously worked as a team, but today they were on different jobs. Clara was the more traditional Nubile Nun, who would doubtless strip down to her wimple for the amusement of some City whizzkid. Rebecca, more unusually, was an

162

LBT – a Loud Blowsy Tart, normally an evening job guaranteed to embarrass you in front of your wife and friends at a night out at the theatre or similar.

But the star of the show, or at least the back seat of Armstrong, was Simon the Stripping Sexton. In his time, he had been billed as the Sex Ton (geddit?), Simon Smith and His Amazing Dancing Bare and, until his credentials were exposed, even the Randy Rabbi. He had also been a talented professional wrestler (i.e. a good actor) in his youth, and still gave the impression that he could look after himself if pushed around. Or pulled around, or fondled, or goosed.

Rebecca's Loud Blowsy Tart was the longest 'act,' so we dropped her off first at a wine bar near St Paul's. Before she got out, she took a small bottle of Gordon's gin from her huge, red-plastic handbag and sprinkled most of it over her neckline and cleavage. Then she carefully nicked another hole in her red fishnet stockings and, once on the pavement, readjusted the seams so they were nicely crooked. Then she tottered off on her four-inch heels. Ah, I love a professional.

I had to drop Simon at Bill Bentley's, the wine and fish bar near the Stock Exchange, and then Clara at a pub in St Mary Axe. The order of pick-up was Simon, Clara and lastly Rebecca. Or to put it another way: a nude (bar the dog-collar) clergyman, a semi-undressed nun and a loud, blowsy tart fighting a losing battle to stay inside a Marks & Spencer blouse at least two sizes too small. And as part of the deal, I had some petty cash with which to buy them all sandwiches and coffee, so they could get changed or dressed while they ate and I took them to the next job, if they had one, or wherever they wanted to go.

I'd got an assortment of sarnies and some cans of Diet Coke and bottles of Perrier at a café behind Liverpool Street and was allowing plenty of time for the traffic to get back into the City. It was just as well. I was idling Armstrong outside the National Westminster Tower – you know, the building that King Kong would have climbed if he'd been British – when the cops pulled me in. Five minutes later, I would have had to explain a naked vicar as well.

It was an ordinary bobby on foot patrol, who strolled out in front of Armstrong and put a hand on the roof after indicating to me to lower my window.

'Are you the owner of this vehicle, sir?'

I wish I had a pound for every time I'd been asked that.

'Yes, he's mine. AJW 440Y.' Before you ask.

'Very good, sir. Now would you mind calling round at Love Lane police station. You

164

do know the way, do you?'

'I could always ask a policeman,' I said before I could stop myself

'And I'd always ask a cabbie,' he said, climbing into the back seat.

Behind us, an impatient motorist tooted a horn. The copper glared out of the back window at him.

'I was thinking along the lines of getting there today, sir, if you don't mind.' You can always tell you're getting old: the policemen get more sarcastic. 'You weren't by any chance waiting for a fare, were you, sir?'

'A fare? This is a private vehicle, officer, unless you're commandeering it.'

'Nothing like that, sir. It's you that's wanted down at the station, and it was kind of you to give me a lift. Anyway, we couldn't leave this – vehicle – here, could we? That'd be a traffic violation.'

Love Lane (what a place for a cop shop!) wasn't actually the nearest nick to where we were, but I didn't think about that. I just concentrated on driving very, very carefully.

'My name is Malpass. I can't believe yours is Fitzroy Maclean Angel.'

'I'm afraid it is.' God knows what had possessed me to put my proper name on my real driving licence, but once it goes into the DVLC computer, it stays.

'What do normal people call you?'

'Mr Angel–' no, don't be cheeky, '–or You There or Buggerlugs – but mostly Roy.'

'Well then, Roy, let's try and keep this friendly.' He was a good six inches taller than me, which isn't saying that much, but a lot heavier, twice as wide and maybe ten years older. He was also, so he said, a detective-inspector in the CID. If he wasn't, he was a bloody good con man and had rented out an office in Love Lane nick under false pretences. It was a standard interview room, and the only non-regulation items to break the monotony of tube-legged table and chairs were the cigarettes, lighter and an ashtray advertising Tuborg lager, which Malpass had placed in front of himself. Even policemen pinched ashtrays, it seemed.

'Is that your cab outside, laddie?' He lit up a cigarette and moved his mouth around as he inhaled, as if chewing the flavour of the smoke. There was a hint of Scottish accent in the voice. And maybe just a hint of Scotch on the breath? Be careful, old son.

'Yes. What's the problem?'

'But it's not a cab, is it?'

'It's a de-licensed cab, run as a private vehicle. Is there any problem here, In-spector? I mean, nobody's said anything to me.'

'No, it's not the cab, Mr Fitzroy, so much as where it's been.'

I almost rose to the bait. It's an old

lawyer's trick to get people rattled by getting their name wrong, if ever so slightly. No, keep cool, baby. It couldn't be about the fire-damaged gin. We'd used Dod's van for that, not Armstrong.

'I don't understand, I'm afraid.'

'And I don't understand how the registration papers, which we so carefully prised out of the Department of Transport's computer in Swansea or some other God-forsaken place, *and* your driving licence, both have an address in Southwark. I don't understand, because the address does not exist any more.' He inhaled smoke deeply and looked me in the eyes. 'The house in question appears to have blown up over a year ago.'

'Faulty gas main,' I said, but it sounded weak.

'So I'm told, but it still means you've got iffy papers on this cab of yours, doesn't it?'

'I suppose so.' He blew smoke at me. Tough guy. 'But I wouldn't have thought that was any call for the serious crimes squad. Do you want me to say that it's a fair cop or something? I forgot. I'll get it done. Okay?'

He leaned way back so that only two legs of his chair touched the floor. It was a trick I'd learned never to do without a crash helmet.

'If you'd done your legal duty, my lad, we wouldn't have had to go through the bother of pulling you off the street,' said Malpass

167

with a sickly smile. 'We could have come round and had a chat instead of having every foot patrol and panda car in the bloody Met wandering around checking the numbers on every pigging black cab in town. In a way, you were lucky young Mason spotted you. He's keen, that lad. Just what were you doing in Threadneedle Street anyway? Meeting your broker?'

'Look, Inspector, just what's going on? I was waiting for a friend, and I would like to get out of here some time this week.'

Malpass thudded the chair forward and leaned over the table. He put his arms out in front, and the hands formed fists.

'All right, Mr Angel. What were you doing outside Sedgeley House on Sunday night?'

I had to admit to myself that that threw me for the minute. Of all the things I'd got up to in my time, I never thought I'd be stitched for trying to return someone's stolen property.

'Called to see a friend,' I said with a dry mouth.

'Got a lot of friends, haven't we? Any friend in particular?'

He beamed innocently, and as his eyebrows went up, I noticed his hairline. He would be bald before he was 50; but I didn't think now was the time to tell him.

'A girl. A girl I met at a party on Saturday night.'

Always tell the truth; not necessarily all of it, though, nor all at once. (Rule of Life No 5.)

'Would that be Josephine Scamp? Mrs Josephine Scamp?'

'Yes.'

'Why?'

'See her, take her out for a drink.'

'Did you?'

'She wasn't in.'

'Been there before?'

Careful. He's probably talked to the old night porter.

'Yeah, once before – last year some time.'

'Know her well?' Now what does that mean?

'Met her two or three times. Socially.'

'Know her husband?'

Here it comes. Don't tell me her old man's a copper and this is one of his mates warning me off.

'No.'

'Know who he is?'

'No idea. You going to tell me?'

'Did you get the feeling at any time that Mrs Scamp was frightened of her husband?'

Oh my God, he's done her in.

'No. It was not something we talked about. Not that we talked much about her ... private life.'

'So you wouldn't know what she's been doing this week.' This was not a question.

169

'I haven't seen her since Saturday, and then only briefly.'

'And exactly where and when was that?'

He produced a notebook and took down the address of the party in Fulham (as best as I could remember it) and the time, which I guessed at around 11.15 pm.

'Can you be more specific?'

'11.16 pm?'

He ignored that and put the notebook away.

'And how long was she there?' he continued, unperturbed.

'Ten minutes, no more.'

'And you've not seen her since?'

'No.'

'Phoned her?'

'No.'

'Romantic sod, aren't you. If she gets in touch with you, tell her to ring this number.'

He took a square of white card from his pocket and flicked it across the table. There was a London phone number printed on it, nothing else.

'The officer at the desk will see you on your way out.' I must have looked puzzled. 'To help you fill out the forms for your cab, so we have your current address. Problems?' He stood up.

'You wouldn't consider giving me a clue as to what this is all about?'

He thought for a moment.

'No.'

He picked up his cigarettes and lighter and left the room. I was dismissed.

I borrowed a ballpoint from the uniform at the front desk and did the honest thing with my address, consigning myself to the bowels of the Driver and Vehicle Licensing Centre's billion-shilling brain down in Wild West Wales.

I had more or less finished when the copper who had pulled me appeared from the back office and lifted the flap in the desk to get by me. I nodded recognition.

'No chance of a lift again, eh?' he said jovially.

'No chance. I'll be getting a reputation as a Black Maria if I'm not careful.'

He shrugged and adjusted the chinstrap of his helmet.

'I'm back on, Trevor,' he said to the policeman at the desk.

'Okay, Geoff. Go down to Bank tube station, will you, and have a butcher's.'

'What's up?'

'Probably nothing. Probably some little pillock stockbroker on the pop. You know, one of the Fizz Kids liquored up and pissing around.'

'Disturbance?' asked Geoff, opening the station door and speaking over the back of my head.

'A streaker. Woman just phoned in, said

she saw a nude vicar, would you believe it, wearing a dog-collar and an early edition of the *Standard.* Heading for the Central Line...'

Oh God, Simon. I'm sorry.

I managed to get to the wine bar the other side of St Paul's in time to pick up Rebecca, and the bar staff did not seem sad to see her go. I told her what had happened, and she took it all in her stride. Once she'd stopped laughing about Simon, she told me to head for the pub where I'd dropped Clara. I said that she must have done her act by now, but Rebecca said not to worry and that she and Clara always followed Plan B – to hide in the Ladies – if anything went wrong.

Sure enough, Clara was sitting at the bar sipping orange juice, her nun's habit wrapped around her, poncho style, just covering her black, lacy basque and suspender belt. If she didn't move suddenly, nobody could spot anything unusual. I mean, nuns have to drink somewhere.

All things considered, I reckoned two out of three wasn't bad. Not that the senior management of Even Rudergrams saw it that way, of course, and it took nearly an hour's arguing before I got about 60 percent of my agreed fee. I was about to leave when the office got a reverse-charges call from Simon, a very angry Simon, in a call-box outside Leytonstone tube station. For the other 40 percent, I offered to go and collect him, and as there were no other takers, I got the job. Actually, Simon took it all rather well and saw the funny side of things. After all, he'd run twice around the Stock Exchange and travelled over six stops on the underground stark naked with no aggro. I'd got arrested (well, virtually) just sitting in a traffic jam.

By the time I got him home to Walthamstow, it was nearly 5.00 and the rush hour was warming up, so it was nearer 6.00 when I got to Stuart Street.

I had intended to try and ring Jo as soon as I got in, to find out what the hell was going on, but I never made it, for the house was in turmoil.

Or to be more accurate, Fenella was in a Turmoil because Lisabeth was in one of her States.

Fenella was half way down the stairs to meet me before I had my key out of the front door.

'Angel, you've got to talk to her – you've got to tell her you forgive her, She's being impossible, absolutely unbearable, and only you can make her come out.'

'Come out of where, Fenella dearest?' I said, putting an arm around her shoulders.

'Your toilet – bathroom, I mean – she's locked herself in. Two hours ago. And it's all because of me.'

Why me? Pulled in by the cops, having to rescue a naked vicar, and now it looked as if I was going to have to talk down a paranoid lesbian.

'What's she on?' I asked Fenella, guiding her upstairs. 'Has she been taking pills or sniffing any...'

'Oh, it's nothing like that, you galoof.' She punched me lightly on the chest. Now I was galoof as well. 'She's just dying of embarrassment.'

'She's done something to Springsteen?'

'No.' Fenella looked genuinely shocked. 'She wouldn't dare!'

I wouldn't have put anything past her, personally.

'Your parents, then?'

'No, thank heavens. They're out. They've gone to a matinée of *Starlight Express*. I've seen it.'

Oh well, that was a relief.

'So where's the problem?'

'It was this friend of yours who turned up this afternoon. He was ever so rude, I must say, and he tried to push his way into the flat.'

'Your flat?'

'No, yours. I don't know how he got in the house, but suddenly he was knocking on your door. I was visiting Lisabeth, you see, while my parents were out.'

We were outside the door by now. It was open and I could see inside, and the closed loo door took on the semblance of the Berlin Wall.

'You said a friend of mine called. Did he say who?'

'No, he just kept asking for you and swearing a lot. He was ever so big and he wore a dinner jacket. That's why Lisabeth thought he might be a musician or maybe somebody giving you work or something. That's why she's so upset about what she did.'

'And just what did she do that was so terrible?'

Fenella took a deep breath, and I noticed for the first time just how impressively she could breathe.

'Well, you see, it was partly my fault, because I just kept saying you weren't in and he got very abusive because he didn't believe me. And then Lisabeth came to see what the noise was and he must have thought she was you for a minute – we had the curtains drawn, you see. Well, the blinds, actually, 'cos you don't have curtains.'

'Yes, yes, get on with it.' What had they been doing?

'Well, this big chap sort of pushed me out of the way a bit. It didn't hurt, honestly, but it looked worse than it was and Lisabeth sort of saw red.'

'What did she do to him, Fenella?' I put

on my stern voice so I wouldn't giggle.

'She kicked him – in the place which is most sensitive.' She'd obviously thought carefully about that.

'And?'

'Well, he doubled up and went quite green. I've never seen that happen before. I thought it was just something people said, but he actually went green, and I thought he was going to be sick. Then he sort of pirouetted, still ... er ... holding himself, and then he fell over and rolled down the stairs. All the way to the bottom.'

Jesus, that was 24 steps. I knew, because I'd climbed them drunk before now.

'He was all right, though,' Fenella said seriously. 'I mean, he got up and walked away. Well, limped, actually.'

I had to laugh. 'Oh dear, poor Nevil.'

It had to be Nevil, from what Bunny said yesterday and Fenella's description.

Nevil had my address.

Why the fuck was I laughing?

CHAPTER TEN

That settled it. There was no way now that Fenella was going to get my body, no matter how much she begged, not as long as Lisabeth was on same continent. Maybe, when Lisabeth had been forcibly retired to some maximum security retirement home in Frinton (as the sign said: 'Harwich for the Continent; Frinton for the Incontinent'), then I'd consider it. Even then, she'd probably manage to mug me with her walking frame.

It took me nearly 20 minutes to talk her out of the loo, finally having to promise that Nevil was not a friend, that he wouldn't call the police, and that there would be no need for Mr and Mrs Binkworthy to know anything untoward had happened that afternoon.

Fenella offered to make her some hot, sweet tea and fetch some chocolate biscuits from downstairs to comfort her. Lisabeth was really into chocolate rushes, and while she fed her face, nuclear war could break out and she wouldn't pause between nibbles, so this gave me a chance to plan my campaign.

That took about three seconds. On the

one hand, I'd been pulled by the cops for reasons that were not yet clear but had something to do with enigmatic Jo Scamp and her gaff in Sedgeley House. And on the other hand, a gorilla in a Top Shop suit called Nevil was looking for me, though he hadn't bargained for Lisabeth's own version of the Neighbourhood Watch Scheme.

Connections: I'd seen Nevil at Sedgeley House; I'd seen Jo at the Mimosa Club, where Nevil was supposed to work, or at least beat up barmen. The Old Bill was interested in Jo; Nevil was interested in me. They both knew where I lived.

The whole thing was like watching snooker on a black-and-white telly. You know it's all a load of balls, but you can't work out who's doing what to whom. And so, having carefully assessed the pros and cons (mostly cons), the solution was clear: do a runner.

While Lisabeth was mainlining Cadbury's Bournville, I rummaged around for a sports bag (one that advertised Marlboro fags, naturally) and began to pack a spare everything. (Rule of Life No 6: be prepared to survive on one extra pair of socks and knickers and a spare shirt. There are always launderettes and it could lead to a career in pop music.)

From the bathroom I took a battery-operated razor, the toothpaste and a new toothbrush from my emergency supply still in their

Sainsbury wrappers. I always keep a few in stock (Rule 17A); they're cheap enough and ever so impressive in the morning-afters.

Then I sneaked my special edition of Brogan's *History of the USA* into the loo and spun the combination. The emergency stash stood at £200 in fivers, and that went into a back pocket. I also removed a building society book in the name of Francis Maclean, which I reckoned had about £450 in the account, and an Access card in the same name that I rarely used and certainly had nearly a grand's worth of credit on it. Along with cash in hand, and the rent being paid up for a month, that should be travelling money enough.

Just in case real travel was in order, I took my passport (real name) and spare driving licence. I also packed Jo's credit cards in the zip pocket at the end of the bag.

By the time I reappeared, Lisabeth had cheered up enough to smile weakly, having adopted the invalid-on-the-sickbed routine. Some invalid. Nevil was probably in traction.

'Binky's just popped downstairs,' she said bravely. 'Her parents are back. Are you going somewhere?'

'What?' I stared stupidly at the bag in my hand as if it had just been dropped there from a helicopter. 'Oh, yeah. I've been invited down to Plymouth for a party at the weekend.'

'It's Wednesday,' she said suspiciously.

'It's going to be a good party.' I picked up my fur-lined leather jacket from the back of the chair and zipped myself into it. 'You don't mind looking after the place for a few days, do you?'

'Well, no...' she said thoughtfully. 'But what about...?'

'The bloke who came visiting? Don't worry. I'll call in and see what he wanted before I go,' I lied. 'Be careful of him, though, he's a bit of a loony. Definitely two bricks short of a wall.'

'You're sure he's not a friend, or anything? I mean I'd hate to have...'

I'd never seen Lisabeth so sentimental before. She needed some iron in her soul.

I sat down on the sofa next to her and patted her hand. 'He's a nasty piece of work, and if he comes back, you treat him just the same as this afternoon. He has a nasty track record, you know. He follows young girls home from school, and one of these days...'

Lisabeth's eyes clouded and I knew I'd done enough. If Nevil did come back, even if he was giving away religious tracts, she'd castrate him before the doorbell had stopped ringing.

I stood up and patted my pockets to make sure I had keys, wallet, and so on.

'What about your lady-friend?' Lisabeth asked.

'Which one?' I said before stopping myself. One had to be careful with female chauvinist sows like her.

'Mrs Boatman or Brightman. She rang again this morning. Didn't Binky tell you?'

'No.' Oh dear, Fenella was going to have the back of her legs slapped again. 'She must have forgotten in all the excitement.'

'Well, anyway,' Lisabeth went on grumpily, 'she did ring and she wants you to get in touch with her at the local National Insurance office. At least I think that's what she said.'

'No problem, I'll bell her tomorrow.'

I said I'd see her after the weekend and shouldered my bag.

Springsteen was sitting on top of the stereo stack, looking out of the window into the darkening sky. I have this theory that at such times he's communing with the mother ship that gave him his mission on this planet, but then I could be wrong.

I playfully tickled him behind an ear and he lazily turned his head and sank a canine into my thumb. It was nice to know I'd be missed while I did a Roland.

Roland? A Roland Rat. I was going underground.

There was nobody out in the street looking suspicious. Well, there were the usual inhabitants, of course, but nobody with the collar turned up reading a newspaper under a streetlamp, say.

I threw my bag into Armstrong's boot and checked the sleeping-bag I always kept there in a polythene bag. While I felt to see if the damp had got to it, my hand strayed over Armstrong's tool kit. A little bit of insurance, perhaps? Better to be safe, and all that. So I removed a rubber-handled wrench from the tool kit – a souvenir of a summer working on rich people's yachts in southern Ireland – and weighed it up and down a couple of times. As I couldn't take Lisabeth with me, it was the nearest thing I had to a lethal weapon.

I pushed the wrench down the side of Armstrong's driving seat and wound up the engine. There was little traffic down through Shoreditch, and I was pretty sure I wasn't being followed, though following a black cab in London must be a pretty thankless task. Having said that, in some of the bits of Shoreditch I passed through, I stuck out like a sore thumb. I mean, Armstrong was the only vehicle with all its wheels left on. At Old Street, I passed the Gym 'n' Tonic health club – I'd been a member there until an embarrassing incident one evening in the female Jacuzzi – then turned up towards Islington proper.

The house where Trippy was squatting was a two-up, two-down terrace cottage with a basement. It was actually a cellar, but London's estate agents removed that word from the dictionary long ago. The squatters had made four bedrooms out of it, keeping the kitchen at the back, and a pretty basic bathroom tacked on to that, as communal areas. Trippy occupied the front ground-floor room, and a local Islington councillor lived in the basement. Who stayed upstairs I never did find out, but the house is now well and truly yuppified and owned by a couple of actresses from good families. (I'm quite fond of them, which is why I'm not giving the address. Actually, it was me who put them on to the place.)

Trippy was in and not at all surprised to see me; but then, very little can surprise Trippy any more. Anyone who once thought a 73B bus was a giant blue salamander following him down Baker Street is living proof that you shouldn't mess around in the medicine chest. (The 73B doesn't even go down Baker Street.)

'Hi ... er ... Angel,' he said fuzzily. 'Is there a gig on?'

'No, it's not work, old son, I've come to crash on your floor for a couple of nights.'

'Fair enough. Come in.'

He led me down the hallway and into the communal kitchen.

'Just having a cook-up,' he sniffed, reaching for a pot bubbling on the gas stove.

183

Trippy constantly snuffled; a bad case of druggie pneumonia, as it's known on the street. Judging by what he was cooking, his sense of smell had gone as well. 'Are you in for a bite?'

I hadn't eaten and was quite peckish.

'No, thanks, I was going to suggest we zip out for a curry.'

'This is curry,' he said, hurt. 'Tricky fella, Johnny Curry.'

He sipped some from a wooden spoon and stained part of his wispy beard a bright orange. Then he turned the gas off and poured the contents of the pan into the big metal bin that seems to be compulsory in vegetarian kitchens and that always contains enough mushy peas to drown a Rugby League team.

'Taj Mahal or Jewel in the Crown?'

'Is there a difference?'

'The Jewel does Kingfisher lager.'

'Say no more.'

Trippy didn't ask any nasty questions. He didn't ask any questions, full stop. That's why I find Trippy refreshing, as long as I'm upwind. But after the cauliflower curry, a couple of pounds of onion rings and six bottles of Kingfisher, I told him that I needed a place to stay out of sight for a few days. That was fine by him as long as I didn't mind sleeping on the floor. I said I didn't, and also, no, I was not short of cash – or at least not short enough to get involved in Trippy's own line of import/export.

Trippy was not really interested in my financial situation; he was just checking that I was paying for dinner. I did so, and I was the one who bought the half-bottle of brandy at the off-licence on the way back.

Well, Trippy said he slept better after a nightcap. I could see why. During the night, three people came into his room from various parts of the squat – or maybe off the street – looking to score. Only two of them fell over me in the sleeping-bag.

The next day started better than it should have.

My aching back woke me around 7.30, but that gave me plenty of time to use the communal bathroom and kitchen. I needn't have worried. I think the next person in the house to leave their pit made it just in time for *Play School*.

There was a local Patels open and doing good business at the end of the street, and I stocked up on orange juice, a couple of meat pies and a packet of chocolate biscuits. These would be my iron rations for a hard day's cruising the streets in Armstrong.

I didn't know where Bill Stubbly lived, but I did know his routine, and he seemed a far better bet than approaching Nevil direct. I mean, he was about 20 years older, two feet shorter and ten stone lighter than Nevil. That made him just about my size.

However odd Stubbly's behaviour had been just lately, I was relying on his basic Northern canniness to keep to some vestige of normalcy when it came to money. Thursdays had always been bank day for Bill. It had been a topic of some concern, in the days when I worked fairly regularly at the Mimosa, that Stubbly always preferred to walk through Chinatown to the Piccadilly Circus Barclays, as even on a Thursday morning he could have got mugged. Not that we worried about that *per se*, but he could have been carrying our wages.

I parked Armstrong in Golden Square, which is known as On Golden Pond to those who work in the posh offices there, and cut through Brewer Street. There were some early tourists about, and they were easy to spot. They hit Laura Ashley's first thing and then see the signs pointing to Carnaby Street (yes, folks, the '60s, like head lice, are coming back) as if it was an ancient monument. I suppose it is, from what I've read about it.

Stubbly was more or less on cue. I was window-shopping across the road at Tower Records (good selection, but top price) when I saw him in the reflection. When I was sure he was alone, I followed him into the bank, and while he queued, I read a leaflet to see if I qualified for a home mortgage. (I didn't.)

By the time he took to do his business, the bank's video cameras must have had me down as a fairly suspicious character, and I was happy to stop fidgeting when he finally turned away from the cashier and headed for the door. He was stuffing a thick wad of notes into his inside jacket pocket as he did so, and I wondered briefly why Stubbly wanted all those French francs; but then, that wasn't any of my business, was it?

'Hello, William, old son,' I said cheerily.

'Bloody Nora,' he spluttered, slapping a hand to his wallet. 'Don't creep up on people like that, specially not in a bank, for Christ's sake.'

I held the door for him on to the street.

'You're getting too set in your ways, you know. That could be dangerous at your age.'

'From what I hear, it could be dangerous being your age,' he said shiftily, avoiding my eye.

'And just what do you mean by that?' I asked, stepping sideways to avoid a brace of female traffic wardens and smiling my best smile as a talisman in case they should visit Golden Square. It never does any good, but what the hell else works with them?

Stubbly paused for a moment, then rocked forward on his heels and prodded me gently in the chest with a forefinger.

'Just for once, for p'raps the only time in

your life, take a bit of advice from your elders and betters.' I waited with bated breath. 'Get lost.'

'Get lost? You mean piss off, don't you? I've told you about reading the *Sun*. You really must improve your vocabulary.'

Stubbly shook his head and started walking towards Brewer Street.

'Can you not take just one single thing seriously?'

'Bill, I'll try,' I pleaded, 'but I have to know what the fuck is going on.'

He stopped again, and we had to flatten ourselves against a wall as a Post Office van mounted the pavement to avoid an illegally parked British Telecom van.

'Just what do you think is going on?'

'I honestly don't know, Bill. I'm being hassled by a gorilla called Nevil – somebody I've never even met. And all I know is he's getting literally close to home and he works for you, if you include disabling your barmen in the conditions of employment, that is.'

He looked at me and chewed his bottom lip as if searching for a remnant of breakfast.

'Just go and lose yerself for a week, son. Honestly, it'll be the best for all concerned in the long run. Especially you, young Angel. Just go away for a week – two at the most.'

And then he started to walk away, leaving

me staring at a bare wall. I did a hop, skip and a bit of a jump to get in front of him and put a hand against his chest. Stubbly isn't a big man, and he's unfit and much older than me, but violence isn't my scene. Unless the odds are really in my favour – and I mean hugely so. (An attack from behind in an unlit alley with no witnesses and an Uzi is my idea of a fair fight.)

'Hey, hey, not so fast, Bill. We're talking serious grievous bodily here, maybe loss of life and limb. Maybe mine. I'm interested; you might even say morbidly fascinated. What have I done to deserve it, I ask?'

He made a half-hearted attempt to brush away my hand. 'I don't know what you're on about. I don't want to know. I don't want to see you and, for your sake, don't be seen with me.' He licked his lips and swallowed hard.

'William... William... Come on, loosen up. Why shouldn't I be seen talking to an old mate, eh?'

'Because I'm not frightened of you, my lad, but I'm scared shitless of Nevil. And if he asks me if I've seen you, I'll tell him as fast as I can. You can be sure of that.'

It was nice in an uncertain world to be able to rely on one thing. Stubbly would never need 30 pieces of silver; he'd take a cheque.

'Just tell me why he's after me, Bill, that's

all.' I think I managed to keep the shakes out of my voice.

'I dunno,' he said quickly, 'and that's straight. I really don't.'

'What about Kenny, then? What had he done?'

'Kenny didn't do nothing. He was just in the wrong place at the wrong time, like I am now, so just piss off out of it, will you? Leave me be.'

I didn't.

'No way, José.' I put both hands up this time. 'There's a lot of bad vibes about – both you and at the club.'

'Whaddayoumean? Nothing wrong with the club.'

'Oh, come on, William, you're not exactly doing gangbusters business, are you?'

'I've got problems with the licence,' he said, like he'd rehearsed it. 'So I thought it best to lie low for a while; keep the nose clean by cutting out the rowdies. That's all.'

I didn't like being called a rowdie, but then I didn't exactly have the time or resources to sue for defamation, if that's the legal terminology for someone who slags you off in public.

'That's bullshit and you know it. The Mimosa is going down the pan faster than Dynorod could. You've lost your customers and you've lost Kenny and suddenly you're employing a goon on a free transfer from

Masters of the Universe. What's the crack, eh?'

'Nevil doesn't work for me,' he snapped, truly indignant.

'So what's he doing at the club, then?'

'He has–' Stubbly began to look shifty; that didn't help; he always did look shifty – 'business interests in the club, that's all. Keep away from him, Angel, and keep away from the Mimosa. It's only for a week or so...'

He stopped himself. He'd said too much – and I hadn't even begun to cotton on.

'What's happening next week, then, Bill? Come on, I'm a big boy now, I can hack it.'

Bill made a determined effort to push me aside, and I had to let him. Over his shoulder, I'd seen a pair of beat coppers walking by. The last thing I needed was being branded a mugger.

'Just disappear, will yer,' Stubbly was saying. 'Go away and stay away from me.'

Then, over his shoulder, he added: 'And stay away from the club. And that bloody woman. She's trouble, I tell you.'

Women – trouble? Gee, if only I'd known that earlier in life.

As it was, I almost missed them.

I'd parked Armstrong around the side of Sedgeley House in one of the diagonal streets that run off to the Edgware Road. It was a quiet little street with the obligatory Charrington's pub at the end, one that, like most of the pubs around there, had a Gents down a near-vertical flight of stairs. A damned dangerous architectural feature if you ask me, which added weight to my theory that the pub must have been designed by a feminist with a grudge.

I was munching a meat pie and reading an early edition of the *Standard* when I saw them, and then only because I happened to glance in the mirror.

Nevil was leading Jo by the arm towards a white Ford Sierra. There was no mistaking his bulk, but I could have been fooled by Jo if I hadn't known her. She was doing a reasonable Madonna impression: black leather mini-skirt, black fishnets and ankle socks, black-and-silver high heels. To top things off, she wore the sort of sunglasses most people thought were old-fashioned in 1958 but now cost about 50 quid a go, and nearly a furlong of white chiffon wrapped around her head, snood-like.

They must have come out of a back entrance to the flats, and they were intent on avoiding somebody, although I'd seen nothing suspicious when I'd cruised down Seymour Place. But then that funny copper, Malpass, had known I'd been out front on Sunday. How?

I didn't worry about it; I had some driving

to do. Despite the virtual anonymity of the FX4 cab anywhere in London, I kept a safe distance behind the Sierra as Nevil headed south and then east, crossing the river in Chelsea, then turning east again, running behind Battersea power station.

The cabs were thinner on the ground now, so I kept a couple of cars between us. Once past the Oval, they got even scarcer, and following became more difficult, basically because I didn't know where I was. I'd never really explored the bandit country north of Peckham; but at least there were plenty of vehicles around to cover me. In fact, every second one seemed to be a jobbing builder's pick-up, either a Mazda or a Toyota, loaded with bits of scaffolding and bags of sand. I knew the type: five years of self-employed brickying, then sell up and buy into a pub near Clacton or Southend and spend the summer serving light-and-bitter to self-employed brickies on a day out with the kids from Peckham or Deptford. So forth, so fifth.

At one point, I almost lost them, until I realised that the Sierra had pulled into a garage for gas. I stopped a hundred yards down the road and checked my bearings in the paperback *A-Z* I keep taped behind the sun visor. It didn't help. I still had no idea where we were going, but I kept the *A-Z* up against my face as the Sierra overtook me.

Back in pursuit, I was relieved to see the Sierra turn north-east towards Greenwich and the river again, running by the old dockyards and into Woolwich. Automatically I checked that I had plenty of fuel myself. I mean, this was still virgin territory, there were no tube lines running to this part of the frontier. God – I was sounding more and more like a real North Londoner all the time.

I almost ran up their exhaust pipe as they turned right off Plumstead Road down the side of a school and into the backstreets.

Fortunately, Nevil wasn't looking in his mirror; he had his head out of the driver's window as if looking for a street name. I gave them as long as I dared before cutting up a newsprint lorry and following them. I was just in time to see the Sierra hang a left once over the railway.

I was right to be cautious. The Sierra had parked about a third of the way down the street, so I went on past the junction and ran Armstrong up onto the pavement.

Leaving his engine running, I nipped back to the junction, hugging the side of a terraced house before peering round the corner.

Nevil was holding the passenger door open for Jo, but they seemed to be arguing. He was wearing a grubby trench coat with the collar turned up, so I still could not get a good look at him, but there was no mistaking his dimensions. I reckoned that his neck and my waist measurements just about matched.

He leaned inwards and seemed to lift Jo out of the car with one hand. If he'd wanted to lift the whole car, I think he could have.

On the pavement, Jo shook herself free and smoothed down the front of her leather mini-skirt. Nevil locked the door and slammed it and then indicated to her to lead on. They disappeared into the front garden of one of the houses.

I checked to see if Armstrong was still there and then risked a crouching run as far as the Sierra's tail-lights. If anybody had seen me, they must have thought the SAS was on exercise in the area.

They hadn't gone into a house as I'd thought. They'd gone down a narrow alley-way – up North they're called 'ginnels,' but don't ask me why; I just observe, I don't translate – which led to another alley at right-angles. Running along that were the back gardens of a terrace of houses we must have driven by.

I had left Armstrong too long, and I hurried back, resisting the temptation to damage the Sierra in some small way (just for peace of mind).

Three small black kids had gathered around Armstrong's bonnet and were gazing in wonder at the gently vibrating engine.

'Piss orf,' I hissed at them, and they calmly turned away and continued down the street, convinced I really was a genuine cabby.

The *A-Z* told me that the gardens off the alley belonged to the houses on Lee Metford Road, and there seemed no good reason why Nevil had not just driven straight there. Unless, of course, he did not want to be seen. It was fairly obvious that Jo did not want to be recognised, but then who would, with Nevil in tow?

I turned Armstrong round on his axis and back-tracked until I found Lee Metford Road. The house I was after was on the south side, that much I knew, but it seemed a pretty standard sort of street with terraced houses down both sides, distinguished only by the colours of the front doors where the residents had actually bothered to renew the paintwork. There were a few cars parked, but none with anyone in it as far as I could see.

Still, I didn't risk a second run, and instead I turned left at the end and found myself back on Plumstead Road. I pointed Armstrong westwards, but pulled over near a post office and a couple of shops to have a think.

Two minutes later, I was sure nobody had ever mentioned Woolwich in connection with Jo. She hadn't, Stubbly hadn't and neither had that laid-back copper Malpass. Maybe Nevil lived here, but if he did, why didn't he use the front door?

All I could think of was that I knew that a Lee Metford was the forerunner of the Lee Enfield .303 rifle and almost became standard issue to the British army before WW1. This close to Woolwich Arsenal, it was logical that they should name a street after it.

You see, I know stuff like that. That's why I always win at Trivial Pursuit.

Sometimes I worry me.

CHAPTER ELEVEN

The answer was staring me in the face. She was a very tasty young mum pushing a baby in a buggy into the post office I was parked in front of, on her way to claim her family allowance, no doubt. The baby was just old enough to have allowed Mum to get her figure back, and Mum's tight wool skirt made sure everybody knew she had. She smiled in answer to my naturally inquisitive stare. Maybe Woolwich wasn't such a bad place after all.

But I had no time for that sort of dalliance. I waited until she'd swung her hips down the road before I went in. Despite what I fancied, it was the post office I needed.

A jovial Indian lady struggling to stay inside her sari helped me find the Electoral Register covering Lee Metford Road and I ran a finger down the names to see if any rang a bell. You can find most people that way unless, like me, they don't register to vote. Ah, isn't democracy wonderful?

'Can I help you at all, chuck?' asked the Indian lady in a nasal Birmingham twang.

'Er ... no thanks, love. I'm just looking for some old family...'

Scamp.

Ada Edna Scamp. 23 Lee Metford Road.

'This is up to date, isn't it?'

The postmistress waddled over to my shoulder.

'Oh aye, chuck, at least I think so. There's no much call for it round here, though.' She fumbled a pair of glasses from the folds of her sari and looked down the register. 'Oi think that's up to date, as far as oi can see, that is, chuck.'

She glanced down the list to where my finger was. ''Ere, you're not looking for Mrs Scamp, are you?'

'The name seems familiar. Do you know her?'

She put her hands to her cheeks and rocked her head from side to side.

'That Mrs Scamp is an old witch, I tell you. I come here three weeks ago to look after this place for my brother Rajiv while he does his business accountancy course. Three weeks only, and already I know that Mrs Scamp. In she comes for her pension, takes it without a by-your-leave, then calls me a bloody wog and tells me to go home to where I come from.'

'And what did you say to that?' I asked, smiling sweetly.

'I asked her if she knew how bloody much the train fare to Wolverhampton was.'

In Armstrong's boot, along with the sleeping-bag and other occasional essentials, I keep what I call my cabby's disguise. It's fairly simple: a fawn flat cap and an old, red-and-black pullover with a hole at the elbow of the right sleeve. (That's where a real musher always rests his arm on the cab window-frame during traffic jams.) For winter camouflage, I have an additional item; a sleeveless, quilted shooting jacket that slips on rather like a bullet-proof vest. I like to blend in when I can.

I checked the backstreets to see if the Sierra was still there. It wasn't, so I did another U-turn and cut back into Lee Metford Road.

No 23 had a front garden the size of a Kleenex, which was either badly looked after or was one of the new butterfly sanctuaries Greenpeace were trying to establish. The door was a scuffed and peeling blue, which had probably been painted at least once since the house was built, maybe to celebrate the toilet coming indoors. It had a tarnished brass knocker showing a pixie cobbling shoes and declaring itself to be a present from Cornwall.

I fingered Jo's credit cards, which I'd slipped into a trouser pocket. It was a flimsy pretext and might not get me anywhere, but it was the best I could do at such short notice.

I took a deep breath, pulled the cabby cap down over my eyes and knocked seven bells out of the Cornish pixie.

'Yes? I ain't buying anyfink.'

I'd half-expected the door to be on a chain or to be asked to push some ID through the letter-box before she opened up. You know, the stuff pensioners are supposed to do. This one just flung the door open, and she'd either been standing behind it when I knocked or, more likely, she'd seen me coming. I knew several wrinklies who took hours to find their glasses when it came to signing a cheque but who could see a net curtain twitch three streets away.

'Mrs Scamp? You ought to be careful opening this door to strangers,' I beamed, though I don't know why I was worried. The last time I saw a face like that was in *Macbeth*, and she had sisters.

'I am careful, sunshine,' she said without smiling, then opened the door wider. Behind her in the hallway was a grey Rottweiler no bigger than a pony and no fiercer than a cobra with a hangover.

'Go on,' said Mrs Scamp. 'Make his day.'

I took a step back. With lodgers like Fang there, who needs Neighbourhood Watch?

'Hey, no problem, Mrs Scamp, I'm not selling.'

'You buying? You totting?'

'No.' Did I look like a rag-and-bone man?

I was supposed to look like a London cabby. Maybe she had a point. ''Ere on a mission of mercy, lady. Returning lost property.'

She relaxed fractionally. The dog didn't move, but I kept an eye on it, though she herself was formidable enough. Though she was no more than five feet tall in her carpet slippers, you just knew it would be best not to cross her. She was the sort of Granny who ate bayonets.

'I ain't lost nuffink. You a rozzer?'

Rozzer? Did people in 'Sarf London' still use words like that? Where was Henry Higgins when you needed him?

'Do I look like Old Bill, lady?' I put on the Cockney something rotten. I'd be doing rhyming slang if I didn't watch out. I pulled Jo's drastic plastic out. 'I've found these.'

'What are they?' she asked, screwing up her eyes and reaching into the pocket of her flowery pinafore. 'My specs are inside.'

'They're credit cards...' I started, as planned.

'I can see that,' she snapped. 'I'm not ready for the knacker's just yet.'

'Sorry, Mrs Scamp, but I found 'em on the floor in the back of the cab.' I turned one round. 'There you are, Mrs J Scamp.'

'That ain't me. I'm not Jay anything, I'm Ay-Eee.' She paused, and I could hear her brain cells creaking into action as she reached out a hand covered in enough costume jewellery to make a decent knuckle-duster. 'You'd better come in. There's no point letting the whole street know our business. Stay there, Nigger.'

I don't know about short-sighted, but the old crone was colour blind. The dog was grey. I knew that, as I had no intention of taking my eyes off it.

'In here,' she said, leaving me to shut the front door, then follow her into the front room.

The dog curled a lip at me but made no sound, then took up position in the front room doorway.

'Nigger won't touch you,' said Mrs Scamp cheerily, 'unless you make a move towards me – sudden, like. I call him that so I can shout down the street after him and those bastards in the race relations office can't touch me for it.' She treated herself to a short cackle. 'I enjoy that.'

Thank God we don't have proportional representation in this country. She'd get elected.

The front room was full of everything front rooms were full of when they had the sale after the Festival of Britain. There was a fireplace, now housing an electric fake-log affair, with a mantelpiece. On it were a variety of jugs and china vases from the same school of design as the pixie doorknocker. Behind one souvenir from a day trip to

Brighton was a crumpled 100-franc note. There was nothing wrong with my eyesight.

There was also a pair of blue-rimmed glasses that Dame Edna Everage wouldn't have looked amiss in. Mrs Scamp levered them onto her face and I handed her the Access card.

'No, this isn't Jack's...' she said to herself.

'I'm sorry, missus?' I played it thick.

'It's definitely Mrs Scamp, but it ain't me. Anyway, I've not been in a black cab in years. Them minicab jobs is miles cheaper than your lot. And they come when you call 'em.'

I tried to look suitably aggrieved.

'It must be 'ers,' she said suddenly.

'You said "Jack",' I offered helpfully. 'Could that be Jacqueline?'

'Nah.' The old lady dismissed my pathetic attempts at logic. 'Jack's my son. These'll be 'is missus, silly cow. Left 'em in the back of a cab, did she? Was she with another bloke, eh?'

'I'm sorry, lady, I don't know what you're getting at,' I said, without a word of a lie.

'Jack's wife,' she said with emphasis. 'I told him she was trouser-happy as soon as I saw her, but he wouldn't listen. Infatuated with her, he was; had to have her. She'd be out running up the bills, I suppose.'

'Who ... er...?'

The old woman dropped the Access card into her pinafore pocket and picked up a framed photograph from a small table near the window. She held it out for me to see.

'That's her, ain't it?'

Through a fine layer of dust and a couple of smudged fingerprints, it was easy to pick out Jo, despite her hair being much longer and the unflattering white trouser suit. The guy with her I'd never seen before. He was shortish and wiry and had a straight, thin moustache, and I guessed he was anywhere between 40 and 45. If you couldn't see that they were outside a Registry Office, you might have thought it was a man out shopping with his daughter.

'Yeah, that's the lady,' I said.

'And she with another feller, eh? When she was in the cab?'

I thought quickly. 'She was with a bloke, but not this one…'

'Well, it wouldn't be Jack,' she said quickly, then stopped herself.

'A much bigger bloke,' I went on. 'Really broad shoulders. Huge guy.'

She cracked her face for a while. Once seen, even the briefest description of Nevil seems to suffice, and she recognised it – and relaxed.

'Well, give me the other one,' she said, holding out the handful of rings again. 'I'll see she gets them.'

I made a show of hesitating. 'Well, I really ought to give them to her personally, or send them back to the bank. That's what we're supposed to do.'

'So you can tap her up for a few quid petrol money, eh? Is that the game?'

She made a sudden move towards me and, from the doorway, Nigger started to growl softly. I came round to her way of thinking and handed over the Visa card.

'Didn't consider that for a minute, lady,' I said, playing the part. 'But come to think of it, I have gone out of my...'

She wasn't listening.

'Or maybe you fancied your chances with her, eh?' She was getting shrill and moving closer. I had a feeling that so was Nigger. 'Fancied my Jack's wife, did yer?'

Then she put her hands on her hips and threw back her head. It took me a couple of seconds to realise she was laughing. I hoped Nigger had a sense of humour too.

'Well, you'd be lucky, my lad! She's too stuck up to look for it in the back of a cab just yet, but it'll come to it one day when she gets a few more years on her; even the milkman won't be safe, and she'll be grateful. I warned our Jack, I did. Did he listen? Hah!'

It was a profound philosopher (or maybe *The Hitch-Hiker's Guide to the Galaxy*) who said bad things always happen on Thursdays. Here was the empirical proof: trapped in Woolwich with a geriatric nutter and the Hound of the Baskervilles.

'Look, lady, I've done my bit and I'll be off now.' I edged towards the door.

'You wait till I tell him she's been spending up West. It was up West, wasn't it?'

She moved after me. From the corner of my eye I saw Nigger retreat a couple of paw lengths, perhaps to get a better run at me.

'Well, it might have been. I can't honestly...'

'Spending like there was no tomorrow, I'll bet. Was it clothes? Did she have clothes with her?'

'I think it was more like Sainsbury's, actually...' Christ, what a daft thing to say.

'She always 'ad more clothes than she could wear. Four or five outfits a day, the spoilt bitch. I told 'im he spoiled her and no good would come of it...'

There was other stuff in similar vein, but by this time I had my hand on the Yale latch and was opening the door.

'Fine... Well, cheerio, missus.'

It was then that Nigger decided to get in on the act, and launched himself the length of the hallway.

I was out of the house faster than a rat up a drainpipe, and I'd slammed the door shut before Nigger banged into the back of it. He was so miffed at missing me that he head-banged the door a couple of times, making the pixie doorknocker rattle on its hinge.

That dog had problems, but living there, I could see why.

I didn't hang about getting to Armstrong and getting him started and headed back to Plumstead Road.

Thank God tomorrow was Friday, it couldn't be worse.

Then I was arrested.

They did it very well, that I'll grant them, but then they've had plenty of practice.

An unmarked Ford Escort pulled out from the kerb slow enough to give me plenty of time to ease up and reach for the horn. But the Escort didn't stop, it came on until it blocked the road completely, and before I could react, my door had been pulled open and a warrant card thrust in my face.

One of them sat in the back – again – and made me follow the Escort, but at least this time they were plainclothes men, not uniformed, so my street cred didn't suffer.

We headed back to the dockyards and onto the approach road for the Blackwall Tunnel. I asked the copper in the back if that was where we were heading but he said, 'Just follow,' so I did, and it was.

The old India and Millwall docks are situated on the one huge horseshoe bend in the river. It's a sobering thought that in a million years or so, the Thames will break through somewhere around Poplar High Street and turn it into a proper island. No, it's not a sobering thought, it's a weird one.

Why should I worry about such things? I mean, it's not as if I owned property there.

I followed the Escort through the tunnel, when it hung a left down towards Cubitt Town but turned into Coldharbour and the cop shop there before then.

This time it was a room with three armchairs and a view over the river. There was a table near the window on which were three Carlsberg ashtrays (no wonder you can't find one in a pub) and a pair of professional-looking binoculars. I could see a barge or something out there in the middle of the Thames, but I've never been much good with boats. My experience on Old Father Thames is limited to the *Tattershall Castle* just down the Houses of Parliament. That has the double advantages of being (a) stationary and (b) licensed.

'Don't do it, laddie,' said a voice behind me. 'The drop's not enough to kill you and the water's pig-filthy.'

'I thought there were salmon in the Thames nowadays.'

'Yeah, in tins, from Tesco's.'

'Another illusion shattered. And what have I done this time, Mr Malpass?'

'You tell me, laddie, you tell me.'

He picked up one of the ashtrays and sat down in an armchair, crossing his legs and balancing it on his knee. He fished out a packet of cigarettes and kept them to himself.

209

'You can start with old Edna. What didya make of her, then?'

'Edna who?'

'Oh tut-tut, laddie, my time's valuable, you know. D'you know, it seems like only yesterday we were having one of these happy little talks.'

'It was yesterday.'

'My goodness me, was it really?' he said, laying on the Scottish accent so that it sounded more like Scotch by absorption rather than birth. 'So yesterday we had our chat and today you go social calling on Mrs Edna Scamp, well-known geriatric reprobate and old slag of the parish of Woolwich. That's what I call interesting. Wouldn't you say that was interesting, Mr Angel?'

I put my hands in my pockets and rocked on my heels. I hadn't sat down because he hadn't asked me to. I notice things like that.

'I find a lot of things interesting. The thought of a Labour Government, interstellar travel, Phil Collins writing a song with a comma in it, why there aren't any walnuts inside a Walnut Whip any more. All that, and more, including why I seem to be this month's centrefold in *Police Gazette*.'

'You're a popular laddie, laddie.' Malpass beamed at that. I suspected that he didn't laugh much, probably on religious grounds. Something to do with the Kirk, and I don't mean Captain James T.

'But let's cut the crapola, shall we? What were you doing with our Edna, eh?'

'How did you know I was there?' It was worth asking. He wasn't going to tell me anything, so I tried to trade info.

'Like the Listening Bank, sonny, we have branches everywhere.'

'That's a relief, I thought you were going to say, "Ve ask ze questions," and then whip the rubber truncheons out.'

Malpass put the fingers of his right hand on the chair arm and pressed them down one at a time until all four knuckles cracked loudly. When he'd done that, he took the cigarette out of his mouth, tapped some ash off and studied the glowing end. I think he'd been practising his pauses.

'We don't need the truncheons, Mr Angel, do we? Because you're going to cooperate with me.'

'I always like to help the Thin Blue Line,' I smiled, not adding that in Brixton it was called the Thick, etc.

'You're bright, laddie, try and catch on. I said help me, 'cos this is a bit personal.'

Oh God. A policeman with a problem I needed like a politician wants a lie-detector test.

'And you're going to help me.' That wasn't a question, and I was getting an awful bad feeling about this. Deep in my stomach the whirling pits started a few trial revolutions, and it wasn't down to the meat pie I'd had.

'Gonna tell me how?'

Malpass stubbed out his cigarette.

'Let me tell you why. First off, you drive a cab but you're not a licensed Hackney Carriage.' Well, I park in Hackney, but it probably doesn't count. 'And we can make life very difficult for you. Give somebody a lift and take cash for it and we've got you, so you might have to be very careful who you travel with, if you get my drift.'

I did.

'Then there's a small matter of your presence at two locations within a week that have been under police surveillance. That's going to take a bit of explaining, I'm sure. But best is last, as we've got you bang to rights handling stolen property.'

If he expected me to break into tears and confess, then he was a good judge of character, but I had Dod to think about, and Dod had a missus and kids and anyway was bigger than me and after all was a pretty good drummer. I should have known. Fire-damaged gin! What an airhead!

'Bang to rights, eh?' was all I could think of to say.

'Yup,' drawled the detective. 'We have a signed statement from a Mr Nassim Some-thingorother to say that–'

Nassim? What the hell had he got to do with it?

'–he accepted the notes in good faith from you as payment for rent on–'

'Pardon?'

I sat down on the edge of the table. Malpass didn't seem to mind. Well, at least he didn't hit me.

'Your rent money, sonny. Two hundred sovs in marked notes. It was hot money – nicked from a sub post office in Southend three weeks ago. We wouldn't have got onto it except it happened to be a post office where the little old lady is careful and takes a note of the numbers of anything over a fiver. All your twenties were on her little list, and when Mr Nassim put them in the bank yesterday, he got a nasty shock. Mind you, so did we when we went round your place last night and found you gone. So it was decent of you to show up today.'

'I don't know where the money came from,' I said feebly.

'No, of course you don't. It just gets left on the doorstep with the milk, doesn't it. Grow up, laddie, this is serious. We have good reason to believe that the Southend job was one of a string of maybe six post-office robberies. Total amount missing is close on 15 grand, and yours is the first to turn up.'

'And if you thought you could pin it on me, you'd have had me cautioned and the bracelets on by now,' I said bravely.

'Quite right, laddie, but I think handling should be enough to hold you for a while. Shall I get one of the uniforms in and take a statement? Do you want to call a brief?'

So, stakes were raised. Well, there's a time to call a bluff and a time to fold – fold up, roll over and beg for mercy, that is.

I told him that Jo had given me the cash, though I was suitably vague as to exactly how I recovered her lost property. I told him that I'd seen her in the company of a minder I didn't like the look of and that I'd followed them to Woolwich. They'd visited the old Mrs Scamp and then so had I, and all I'd found out was that she was Jo's mother-in-law and probably had a picture of Hitler on her bedside table.

'How did they get in?' was all Malpass asked.

'In the back. There's an alley running along the back of the gardens. They parked round the corner.'

'Bugger,' he said softly, to himself.

'You didn't have anybody watching the back, did you? Just on Lee Metford Road, and all you saw was me.' Why was I so smug about that? After all, I was the one in trouble.

Malpass brought out his cigarettes again and this time offered me one. I broke the filter off and tapped it on my thumb before I took a light from him. Joe Cool hisself, I don't think.

'Manpower, you see. It all comes down to manpower. Not a big enough allocation for something like this, that's the trouble.'

'I'd think 15 grand was a good reason to call out the dogs, or doesn't it work that way?'

'Oh, the Essex lads are out in force, no problem, but I'm sure the hooligans who did the post offices were working from south of the river. That's what the grapevine says, and I think I know why.'

'But you don't really think it was me?'

He smiled the way the German general von Moltke smiled when the Swedish ambassador told him Stockholm was impregnable.

'No, I don't think you knock over post offices. In fact, I don't really care who actually did the jobs at all.'

'Now there's a novel approach to police work. I bet it keeps the filing easy.'

'Don't be lippy. I don't like it, and it'll annoy me now we're working together.'

'I don't like the sound of that.'

'That's only 'cos you don't know what you're into. You're surprisingly innocent.'

'I bet that's not said much round here.'

He let that one go.

'What you have wandered into, sonny, is a private feud. I'll be honest with you, it's very personal business, which is why I need you, but by Christ you need me.'

'Go on,' I said as if I meant it.

'I know old Mother Scamp from way back, you see, and she's a bad 'un. Always was. Small-time South London villains have a habit of getting above themselves, and they usually come a cropper when they tangle with the East End families or the heavy mobs dealing in drugs. The Scamps have always been Third or Fourth Division, but they've spread the work in their time, and that's why old Mrs S is now calling in the favours.'

'You mean that white-haired old lady? Maybe she diddles the Meals on Wheels people, but masterminding a string of robberies?'

'Oh yes, I'm quite convinced of it.'

'What for? The Whist Drive not exciting enough?'

'Oh, there's method in it. She's raising cash to finance the springing of her son Jack.'

'Springing? As in "from prison"?'

'You're catching on.'

'And when is this supposed to happen?'

'It has. Either late last Saturday or early Sunday morning. Just about the time you've admitted taking two hundred stolen notes from Jack's wife.'

That convinced me. I definitely hated Thursdays.

CHAPTER TWELVE

Malpass suggested we go for a drink. It was 5.30 and the pubs were opening, jovial landlords all over London withdrawing rusty bolts from front doors to greet the homeward throng. If Malpass had suggested a swim round to Mortlake, I'd probably have agreed.

He made me drive, so Armstrong had yet another policeman in the back, and directed me towards Mile End. Limehouse, he said, was full of politicians, and Bow was being yuppified. Only in Mile End, where there used to be a fair crop of breweries, could you find a good pub with a good pint of beer.

We found a pretty hideous street-corner boozer, and Malpass ordered two pints of Charrington bitter.

'I'll be straight with you, Angel, though I still can't believe that's your name.'

'Suspend disbelief, Mr Malpass. I do, quite often.'

He sipped some ale and smacked his lips. 'We're well off the record now, so I'll tell you something about Jack Scamp.'

'This is why it's personal. That it?'

'Yes, but also there are things you should know, as we'll be working together.'

Why did I just know I wasn't going to like this?

'Jack Scamp is a south-of-the-river villain who was never as tough or as important as he thought he was. Not that he's not tough; oh no, it'd be a mistake to underestimate how vicious the little sod can be.'

'You sound as if you've an axe to grind there, Mr Malpass.'

'Not so much grind as bury in the back of the little bastard's head if I get half a chance.' He caught my look. 'Yes, it's that personal. He did something to a friend of mine, two years ago. A young DC just out of uniform, name of Leakey, was getting in close on one of Scamp's sordid little protection rackets. I was supposed to be running the operation, but I got caught up with other business. Too busy to back him up, I was. And so one morning, he's found on a plot of waste land in Dagenham, with both his knee-caps smashed to mush by a cricket bat. A fucking cricket bat!'

'Scamp?'

'Or one of his heavies. Scamp had an air-tight alibi, naturally, but then again, young Leakey never said who exactly had done it. When he got out of hospital, he left the Force. Only walked properly about three months ago. They had to keep ripping the knee-caps apart and rebuilding them. Scamp broke his bones and his mind. His nerve

218

went totally, and now his own shadow scares him shitless.'

'So you feel guilty and you've made Scamp your personal crusade. Is that it?'

He put his face in his beer and finished the pint in one go. I wondered if I was expected to buy the next round as well.

'Well, I don't think of it as a crusade, more a cleansing operation. And, like I said, it is personal.'

'You felt responsible for what happened to Leakey,' I said soothingly. Maybe I'd put in a consultancy bill.

'Oh, I got over that. It's personal because when I heard what had happened to young Leakey, I lost my rag. You should never do that. I went round to Scamp's lock-up ware-houses – he had a couple down in Woolwich in those days – and he wasn't there, so I torched 'em. Helluva blaze. It turned out he was storing paint, among other things. Of course, Scamp gets to claim about 20 grand on some dubious insurance policy, and I resign myself to the fact that I'll never get beyond Inspector. Oh yeah, I've been told as much. My career finished, just because I lose control and take it out on a piece of shit like Jack Scamp.'

He rattled his empty glass, and I half stood to go to the bar.

'So I'm determined to get my own back,' he continued. I sat down. I didn't want another drink anyway. The sod would probably breathalyse me after he'd made me drive him home. 'Some philosopher said revenge is the best way of getting your own back, didn't he? Well, I feel like that. So I've been biding my time. I thought we had him last year when he lost his rag in a pub down in Kent and tried to push a glass through the landlord's face.'

'He sounds a real charmer,' I offered. Malpass's eyes had misted, and I was talking just to remind him I was there.

'Oh he is, sonny, he is.'

'So what happened about the publican?'

'We nicked him, all right. Scamp got two years for assault, grievous bodily, so on, so forth. Pathetic, really, for someone with his record. He could have got away with 14 months with remission.'

'Could have?' I asked quietly, my stomach having suddenly acquired a large ice cube.

'If he hadn't escaped from Her Majesty's Pleasure.' Malpass looked at me, then at his empty glass. 'Last Saturday night, just about the time you were with his wife at that party in Fulham. Didn't you know? It's your round.'

I told Malpass he could find me at Stuart Street and, for a couple of streets, I did head that way. Then I did a couple of dog-legs and turned towards Trippy's squat.

I'd lost my appetite, I didn't want a drink and I was playing Frankie Goes to Hollywood (am I the only one who bought their second LP?) very loudly on Armstrong's in-cab sound system. My mind wasn't on my driving, and for the first time I almost collided with another taxi. It was one of the new, five-seater Metro-cabs, though, so that doesn't count. I realised why people confuse them with hearses.

Malpass had told me a few more bits of the story; not enough to know what was really going on, but just enough to make me feel uncomfortable. It's a knack only policemen, solicitors and builders doing estimates have.

Jack Scamp had drawn a two-year plate of porridge for the assault on the Kent licensee and, as Malpass had said, would have been out with remission, if he'd kept his nose clean, in three months' time. But our Jack hadn't kept his nose clean, being the sort of bloke who was born with somebody else's silver spoon in his fist if not his mouth.

No, our Jacko had thrown a wobbler and gone over the wall. Not a very high wall, at a low-security, semi-open prison in Buckinghamshire. You know, the sort where they do classes in ballistics and Open University degrees in SAS tactics.

The reason he'd gone over the wall was simple. He'd had some bad news brought to him in the nick by his mother, the Wicked Witch of Woolwich. She'd told him that his wife, young Jo, had been carrying on with other men, other women, nuns, rapists, ex-Nazi war criminals, you name it. Jack had, to use a medical expression, gone ape-shit.

Just as he had last year in the pub in Kent when he'd glassed the landlord – when the landlord had chatted up Jo while Jack was in the bog.

You see, Jack Scamp was absolutely stark-staring red-mist fucking paranoid jealous when it came to anyone messing about with his wife.

And he was out of prison.

And he broke bones like other people collect stamps.

And I was supposed to sleep nights?

My mission, should I decide to accept it, was to find Jack Scamp for Malpass before Nevil found me for Jack Scamp. This taxi will self-destruct in ten seconds. Mission-bleeding-Impossible.

The trouble was, it wasn't impossible. I could stake myself out and let Nevil come for me, relying on Malpass and the boys in blue to arrive in the nick of time.

Alternatively, I could find Scamp myself, then stand back and let the cavalry come. Just as dangerous, probably, but at least it might get the whole affair over with and, to some extent, I would be in charge of my own destiny.

Wishful thinking, I thought. Still, the only other option was to disappear off the face of the Earth, and that could involve leaving London. I couldn't do that; I mean, I had responsibilities, and if I had time I'd remember what they were.

I suppose, if the truth was known, I was narked at being pushed around. And you should never do things just because you're angry.

The first move was to set up a meet with Jo.

I wanted her to fill me in on the blank spots, and wanted to hear it from her, not anybody else. There was also the small matter of 250 smackeroos outstanding. And I was looking for real ones this time.

So, into action.

Firstly, I needed a woman. More specifically, I needed a woman's voice, and Trippy's place would have to do.

Plan A almost fell at the first fence, as Trippy and the rest of the squat seemed to have been having an end-of-season sale in Trippy's medicine chest.

They were all sat on the floor of one of the sparsely-furnished bedrooms, the curtains drawn, watching *EastEnders* on a black-and-white telly, and they were eating Greek yoghurt out of a communal, family-sized

Sainsbury's tub. That combination would have softened my mind without recourse to proscribed substances.

There were five of them, I think; it was difficult to be precise in the gloom. I found Trippy by stepping on him.

'Hey, man ... easy. Tread soft.'

I knelt beside him and put my mouth as close to his ear as my nostrils would allow.

'This is Earth calling Starship Trippy,' I said. 'Please respond.'

'Hey, Angel. What's your prob? Wanna snort? Oh, I forgot, you don't, do you?'

'Trippy, I need a woman.' And I wished I'd bit my tongue off.

'Hey – I remember them. They're the curved ones...'

'To make a phone call for me.'

'Well, all right,' he laughed. What could he have suspected?

'Is anyone in the house straight?' I used the term loosely, but Trippy knew what I meant.

'Nicola is,' Trippy slurred. 'Well, fairly. That's why we're having a party; she's got a job.'

I felt a hand on my knee. An attractive young blonde I hadn't seen before was offering me a joint. I smiled and shook my head. I hadn't noticed, but the room stank like a Lebanese spice rack.

'That's Nicola,' said Trippy, so I smiled

again. 'She's worried about keeping her works clean, and we don't have any spare, so she's staying low.'

Well, that was fairly straightforward. Nicola had no clean works – i.e. a fresh hypodermic (the Aids scare has a lot to answer for) – and so was staying on the dope: 'stay low' coming from one of the Government's laughably ineffective drink/driving campaigns.

'Hi, Nicola.'

'Hi.' Nicola sat down on the floor and slowly rolled over onto her back. With more hair, she could pass for Springsteen being playful in the dark.

'So you're the odd one out, eh? The one with the job.'

'Yeah.' Nicola exhaled with her eyes closed. 'Start Monday.'

'Doing what?'

'Social worker.'

I should have guessed.

'You wouldn't like to do a bit of social work for me, would you?'

'What did you have in mind, big boy?'

'Make a phone call for me.'

A tall, thin guy I had seen in the house before crawled on all fours in front of the television to get at Nicola's joint. One of the other zombies threw a shoe at him.

'What's it worth?' said Nicola, ignoring the guy, who was creeping back across the room with her joint in his mouth. Well, I think it was his mouth. It was dark.

'A tenner?'

'I'd settle for a Big Mac.'

'One call and I'll make it a quarter-pounder with fries.'

'Sold – to the man in the Biggles jacket.'

I took stock of my fur-lined leather jacket, which I had prized for years, and I didn't see any problem. George Michael could have got away with it, but then he can get away without shaving. I decided not to rise to the bait.

'Where's the phone, Trip?'

Trippy took an age to sit upright.

'Problemmmmm,' he sighed. 'It's in the basement flat, and our friendly local councillor is out for the night. Flat's closed and locked, man.'

'Yale lock?'

Trippy nodded, then smiled.

'Well, that's never stopped us before, has it?'

I've never trusted Yale locks unless you remember to hit the dead switch, which few people do. You can't blame the manufacturers. Likewise, I've never trusted anyone who says he can turn one over with a piece of plastic or a credit card. In the old days, before machine-made doors and draught-excluders, maybe, but not these days.

I use an old and trusted nail file, one of

those ones with the curled end for digging deep into the cuticle. It's well-worn now, mainly due to being pushed in and out of locks, but you can't be arrested for carrying it. And if you have the knack and a light enough touch, you can just about ease back the spring enough to release the tongue. But why am I telling you all this? Just take my word for it.

It took us about two minutes to get into the basement flat, about five minutes for Nicola to shake off the giggles, and about another five for me to brief her as to what to say.

'Now remember, if a man answers, say you want to speak to Jo. If he says she isn't there, say you'll come round and wait. Just bluff him out.'

'But if this Jo answers, I'm to stick to the script, right?'

'Right.'

And give her her due, she did.

'Hello, is that Jo...? Good, listen, I've got a message from Carol... Yes, Carol Flaxman. She wants to see you tomorrow... No, it has to be tomorrow... Seymour Place baths... Swimming baths... Swimming baths, tomorrow at 5.00... She says she knows it's difficult to get away, but this is really important and if you don't come, then I think she'll gatecrash your place... I know, I know, but you know what she's like... No, I'm just a friend... No... Just be there, five o'clock... No, in the pool, she'll be waiting... Okay, good-bye.'

Nicola hung up the local councilor's phone and ran a hand through her hair.

'How was that?'

'Oscar-winning. What did she say?'

'Well, she didn't like the idea much, but she said she'd try.'

'Great. I owe you a hamburger.'

Trippy began to sniff and hop from foot to foot. He was anxious to get out of the basement and back upstairs. Whether it was because he was a lousy burglar or because he was wasting valuable brain-damaging time, I couldn't tell.

'Let's go, kids,' I chirped.

'Er ... I'd better get back upstairs...' Trippy began.

'Sure, sure,' I said, waving him away. 'Thanks for everything, it was a great help.'

'Oh, yeah, right, good.' He nodded to himself as he climbed the stairs, wondering what he'd helped with.

I didn't have the heart to tell him or Nicola that I was worried that Jo's phone would be tapped. He wouldn't remember, and I hoped she wouldn't ask nasty questions.

'I'll get my coat,' she said.

I must have looked blank.

'So we can go for a Big Mac,' she said as if talking to an infant.

'Right. Great. Let's go.'

She took a couple of minutes to get her coat, wash her face and comb her hair. It really was a pleasant shade of blonde now I looked at it.

'Where are you sleeping?' she asked as we made the front door.

'On Trippy's floor, just for a few days.'

'Is it comfortable?'

We stepped out on to the street and she walked alongside, eyes down, looking at the pavement.

'Much as can be expected.'

'Is Trippy a sound sleeper?' I felt her hand rooting for mine in the pocket of my jacket.

'Like a log.'

'That's useful.'

I'd been right; she wasn't the inquisitive type. But that phone call was going to cost me more than a Big Mac.

Thank God British Telecom didn't send bills like that.

I slept late that Friday. All the stresses of Thursday and then having to entertain Nicola had left me truly cream-crackered. I find that, though. When I have problems, they never keep me awake nights, I just sleep. It must be a sort of mental hibernation, a stress-induced torpor.

We hadn't been disturbed too much by Trippy. At about 2.00 am he had fallen downstairs and slumped in a heap by the front door. Nicola had made me go and see if he was okay and I'd said yes he was, because I'd seen his eye move, and I'd left him there.

Nicola had gone out about 9.00 am saying she had to go on an executive management training course on How to Piss People About in advance of her new job. Would she see me tonight? Maybe. I can be really decisive sometimes.

I frittered away the morning and then got Armstrong wound up and headed towards the West End. I stopped at a pub I used rarely near the BBC and had a ploughman's and a couple of orange juices, no alcohol, partly because I wanted to keep a clear head and partly to fit in with the cab-driver persona.

Then I went shopping down at Lillywhites and bought a pair of swimming shorts, a Speedo swimcap and a pair of swimmer's goggles. There had been no point in looking for a towel at the squat, but I knew Seymour Place baths hired them out. So I was all set.

I still had time to kill, so I thought I'd make a couple of phone calls, and that meant employing the Middleditch gambit.

It's quite simple, really. You pick a big office block that has a reception and preferably a switchboard near the front door. You draw up in your taxi (motorbikes work even better) and park right outside, making sure you are seen by the security man or the receptionist. Then you march in clutching a thick, sealed brown envelope on which is written 'Mr Middleditch – By Hand'. (I carry one ready made in Armstrong's glove compartment.) You announce that you want Mr Middleditch, and when they say there's nobody there of that name, you ask if you can 'ring the office' to find out what's going on. They always let you use a phone, and sometimes you get a private one in a booth or similar, and I've made many Stateside calls that way. I've even been brought cups of tea. One of these days, though, I'll find an office where there really is a Mr Middleditch, and I'll have to leave a well-wrapped paperback edition of *The Story of O*. It might almost be worth hanging around to see him open it.

Anyway, Mr Middleditch came through once more, and I got through to Lisabeth on Stuart Street. She calmly told me that the police had called round and that Nassim had been looking for me. Then she got more excited and told me that a Mrs Boatman had called from the National Insurance and was ever so attractive and charming. Oh yes, and Springsteen was okay but had been sick on the stairs. And no, I shouldn't worry about it as Fenella had cleared it up before Frank and Salome had got home.

I risked another Middleditch and luckily caught Bunny at home. Had he heard any more about the Mimosa Club? No, he hadn't, but as far as he knew there was no music on there still. He was going down to Soho later and he'd look in. Any messages for Nevil? Sod off, Bunny, but don't say that to Nevil.

I waved at the receptionist, who had obviously forgotten about me, as I left, saying: 'Sorry, the despatcher's given me the wrong street.' I haven't paid for a phone call in years.

By 4.30 I was cruising round Seymour Place swimming pool, parking on the blind side as far as Sedgeley House was concerned. I had brought my bag with me, and I left it in Armstrong along with my wallet, spare cash and watch, just taking enough to pay for a ticket and a towel. In case anything went wrong, I was prepared to make a dash for Armstrong. I didn't want to have to hang about waiting for the attendant to open lockers.

With the swimming cap and goggles on, I could hardly recognise myself, certainly not from a distance, and I also intended to be underwater for most of the time. Just to make sure, however, I moved quickly through the showers to poolside and dived in.

I'd got Nicola to say five o'clock because I knew the pool would be busy, with businessmen and secretaries dipping before heading home and a fair smattering of kids getting in practice for the school team. (The synchro swimmers get me. How do they smile with those nose clips on and one leg in the air? Moreover, why don't they drown? I would.)

I did a length just to loosen up, and by the end of it I was desperate for a cigarette. I hadn't realised how out of shape I was getting. Then I slipped over and did a leisurely backstroke back up the pool. This gave me a chance to check out the spectator balconies that overhang the two long sides of the water.

There were no spectators at all, which was a relief, and no-one in the water of a size or shape that could be Nevil. A Great White would have been less out of place.

I was hanging on to the ledge at the deep end, arms out in the crucifix position, when I saw her come out of the ladies' changing rooms wearing a yellow-and-white-striped one-piece. Good choice, the yellow showing off her tan nicely.

She looked up and down the pool, then moved to the edge and trawled a toe to test the temperature to check that it really was the 82° the notice board on the way in had said. Then she turned and walked towards the deep end, turned again and did a perfect back flip, hardly denting the surface and coming up into a smooth breaststroke only a few feet away from me.

Three powerful strokes brought her to the rail, where she went straight into an underwater turn and headed down the pool. She'd been within a yard of me and not recognised me. So far, so good.

I followed her, using a slow breaststroke and keeping my face underwater as much as possible. She made the shallow end and stood up, plastering her hair back with her hands. She almost popped out of the swimsuit as I passed her and said, 'Hello, Jo.'

I turned without stopping and crawled back to the deep end, looking back as I breathed to make sure she was following. She was a good swimmer – better than me – and we touched the rail together.

'I had a funny feeling you'd be around here somewhere,' she said.

'You must be psychic.' I pushed up my goggles to get a better look at her.

'No, I just remembered you mentioned the baths when we first met.'

She trod water slowly, her hands clasped behind her back. You can do that only if you are really relaxed and have a clean conscience.

'Actually, it's your wonderful memory I wanted to talk to you about.'

'I know, I still owe you 50 pounds.'

'250, actually, now the police have it. It's they who are keen for you to remember where you got it.'

She stopped treading water and reached for the rail. She put her head back and looked up at the ceiling.

'Where's Jack?' No reaction. 'He's around somewhere, isn't he?'

Jo put her arms straight up and sank to the bottom, kicked off and came up shaking her head. Thinking time. She still wasn't talking, though.

'Come on, Jo, loosen up. I've been primed with stolen cash from a post-office raid set up to finance your old man's own version of early day closing at the nick. I've been dragged in by the Old Bill twice, and your pet grizzly bear Nevil is making life very uncomfortable for people I know. You got me into this, lady. Help me get out.'

'What can I say? You're over 21. Well over.'

'You know you are being watched.'

'Yes, but not all the time. They haven't got the manpower. Too many villains about.'

That was rich. I began to think she was enjoying this. 'Well, they missed you at Lee Metford Road yesterday.'

That shook her.

'How do you know?'

'I saw you and then I saw Mrs Scamp. She doesn't think too highly of you, does she?'

'I've taken her Jack away, that's why.'

'I thought the High Court had done that.'

She shot me a look, then kicked off from

the wall of the pool, and I followed as best I could. As soon as the water was waist high, she stood and walked to the side near to the female showers. I reached her just as she was about to hoist herself out. I put a hand on her arm.

'Jo, all I want to know is: what have I got into and how do I get out? Life's too short to have to watch your back all the time.'

She put her hands on the side and straightened her arms and held herself there. It's a good trick. She was fit, I'll give her that.

'Just stay away from me, will you? I'll try and get you some cash if that's what worrying you.'

'It isn't. I want to know why Nevil is after me.'

'No, you don't.' She was still hanging there, apparently without strain.

'I'll keep asking.'

'That wouldn't be clever.'

Then she was out of the water, her feet slapping towards the showers.

I got changed in double quick time, but she must have beaten me. There was no sign of her in the entrance foyer, nor in the street outside. I reckoned it would take her three or four minutes to get back to her flat, but maybe it wasn't a good idea to hang around the neighbourhood.

I hurried round the corner to where I'd parked Armstrong and climbed aboard.

I dug a comb out of my bag and adjusted the driving mirror so I could sort out my hair before it dried frizzy.

The mirror was full of a huge, white-shirted arm coming from somewhere in the back seat to encircle my throat.

Nevil had just found me.

CHAPTER THIRTEEN

Nevil choked me until I almost passed out, then he lifted me out of the driver's seat and bundled me into the back of Armstrong, hitting me on the back of the neck with what could have been an anvil but was probably his fist. And then, when I was really unconscious, he poked my eyes out.

Well, that's what I thought when I came round. I couldn't see anything, so it seemed a logical assumption. Then my sense of smell came into play, and I could smell motor oil, and if I concentrated, I could feel the cloth wrapped tightly around my head. Then I began to realise that my hands were tied behind my back and my legs were also secured to something. I thought it might be a chair, but there didn't seem to be a back to it, and it was smooth and cold.

There was no time to think of anything else. The pain in my head came then, and I felt sick. Then I heard somebody say, 'He's come round, Jack,' and the blindfold was ripped away, along with a chunk of hair.

My eyes watered with pain, with chlorine from the swimming pool and with oil from the rag I'd been blindfolded with. Slowly,

Nevil's chest came into focus. It seemed to go on forever. He had his shirtsleeves rolled up and his arms folded like piled-up hocks of ham. On top of a neck the diameter of a drainage pipe was a head with a totally expressionless, moonlike face. I looked into his eyes and they reminded me of the saying: 'The lights were on but there was nobody home.'

Nevil did not look at me, even though his eyes were pointed roughly in my direction. His head was cocked to one side as if awaiting instructions.

I turned my head slowly, and now my throat started to hurt. I wasn't sure I could speak even if I had anything to say.

Jack Scamp was ignoring me, but I had a feeling my luck couldn't last.

He was zipping up a small, brown suitcase, which he placed under the table he was standing at, next to another one. There was not much else to look at in the room. There was one chair, a camp bed with one pillow and one blanket, and several cardboard boxes, some with groceries in, some full of rubbish; beer cans, MacDonald's cartons, and so on.

I tried to swallow and it hurt. I tried to move my hands and they hurt, but I established that they weren't tied, they were taped at the wrists. My feet were secured by a length of electric cable, which could have come from a table lamp. The cold, smooth thing I was sitting on was a beer keg, which explained why my bum hurt as well.

Jack Scamp had a cigarette dangling from the corner of his mouth. He drew on it, then took it out of his mouth and nipped the end off before dropping it on the floor. Prison habits die hard.

I recognized him from the wedding photograph old Ma Scamp had flashed in front of me. If anything, he looked younger and fitter; he'd certainly kept himself in trim, although the hair was thinning and he seemed to be cultivating one long strand on the right side that could be plastered over the scalp. I've always thought that much more undignified than going bald.

He was certainly no taller than me, and he stood in an instinctive boxer's crouch. He was wearing a Levi's sweatshirt and a pair of jeans without showing a belly-bulge between them; something few men over 45 can do.

'I've been looking forward to seeing you,' he said, coming up close so I could smell him. He gave off a mixture of sweat and sex. I've known it happen to people who get excited easily. He probably had trouble with his glands.

'There's been a mistake,' I croaked. 'I don't know you.'

'But I know you, sonny.'

Why do bullies always call people sonny?

240

I'd noticed that with Malpass. And where was he when I needed him?

'I've never seen you before in my life,' I said, not believing for a minute that honesty was going to be the best policy.

'But you've seen my wife, haven't you, you turd.' He yelled this in case I had trouble hearing him from six inches away.

I recoiled so much I thought I was going to topple backwards, but the cable round my legs kept me anchored to the beer keg.

'Thought you could get your slimy little end away with my Josephine, didn't you?'

For a moment I thought he'd flipped and reckoned he was Napoleon, when it clicked he was talking about Jo. I was right about him having flipped, though.

'I don't...'

'Don't what? Don't lie? Don't like women? That's not what I've heard, and I've been asking around about you. You're Jack-the-lad, not me. Nobody's ever called me that. You're the fancy music man, aren't you? The smoothy who drives around in a cab. What sort of a man does that, eh? You're not a kid, you should know better than to sniff round other men's wives.'

Well, this was a turn-up, getting lectured on morality by a South London hood.

'There's one thing I can't stand, and that's messing around with other men's wives. I never did it. I'd never do that to anybody, and I don't like it happening to me.'

He was so close now I could count his teeth. I was seeing his pock-marked face through a red film of chlorine irritation. I could still smell it, and his breath and his sweat. I retched down the front of my T-shirt and Scamp stepped back, but it didn't stop his flow.

'I think about these things all the time, see.' He put a forefinger to his temple to illustrate thinking, just in case I wasn't following.

'I know I have to watch Josephine, because men are always after her.' He began to step from one foot to the other, more like a boxer than ever. 'She can't help it, that's why I have to look after her. That's what I do.' He paused and nodded his head. 'Yeah, that's what I do in life, I look after my own.'

Then he suddenly went up on his toes, and both hands flashed out and clipped me on both cheeks. The blows were not that hard, he hadn't even made proper fists, but by God they were fast.

'Looking after my own, that's what I do,' Scamp continued as if nothing had happened. 'And I do it so that people know I've been around and I've kept my eyes open.'

'You've got the wrong bloke,' I said, tasting blood. My lip, I think.

'Oh no I haven't. Your name is Angel, you're the one with the cab, the one who plays in a band. I know you've been seeing my Josephine and I've heard you brag about it, you cocky little bastard. Now nobody, but nobody, does that to Jack Scamp and gets away with it.'

He was back in front of me, prodding me with a forefinger.

'I have a position to keep up, sonny, and I do it by leaving little messages so that people know I'm on top of the situation. Your friend Kenny was one of my messages, except that Nevil here did that one. He wanted to do you too, on account of what one of your girlfriends did to him.' I heard Nevil breathe loudly. 'But I said no, I had to do this one personally. Bring him.'

Scamp turned to reach down into one of the boxes of groceries that were scattered over the floor, but I didn't see what he was after as Nevil was lifting me up by the shoulders.

He picked me up and clear of the beer keg so that the flex holding my legs came off clear but it stayed on my ankles, acting as a hobble. Nevil just walked with me about a foot off the floor until I hit the table with my stomach.

That seemed to have been what he had in mind, as he put a paw on the back of my neck and bent me forward until my face was squished into the table top.

I felt him rip the tape off my hands, but he

kept my left arm in a hammer-lock. My right arm, he forced around in front of me and pressed it hard onto the table, so that the fingers splayed out just in front of my face.

Scamp came around and stood in my line of vision. The hammer-lock kept my head down, but I could see he was carrying a bottle of whisky by the neck.

'I'm going to enjoy making you one of my messages,' said Scamp. 'As soon as I heard about you, I promised myself I'd make sure you retired early from the orchestra pit.'

He didn't smile, or laugh like maniacs are supposed to. He just smashed the bottle down across my hand. He did it twice before the bottle broke.

I would have laughed, because the fucking loony thought I was a pianist. I would have, if I hadn't fainted.

'No, it is him. I know him, he's a mate, probably just had a few and he's sleeping it off. He won't mind, honest. Come on, he won't...'

I knew the voice from somewhere. It seemed important to remember from where.

Bunny. It was Bunny, my old mate, me auld mucker, my pal, the man I would trust with ... with ... well, he'd have to do.

'He's crook, I tell yer.'

This was another voice, one I didn't know,

and there was something odd about it. It was female, but that was okay, I could remember them. It was also Australian; that was it. Maybe a Qantas jet had landed and the hosties were on the rampage. If they were, Bunny would have found them.

I hauled myself up from whatever I was lying on. It was the floor of the back of Armstrong. Door-handle; that was my next big objective. Now I was really in control.

Tap-tap.

What the hell? Bunny was rapping on the window. 'Hey, Angel, you've got a fare. Let's roll and hit the spots.'

'I'm telling you, he's crook, sick, ill. Strewth, can't you see?'

Good for you, lady. I'll never be sarky about *Young Doctors* again.

'He's had a drink or three, that's all.' Thanks, Bunny, I owe you. 'Come on, Angel-face, open up.'

I grabbed for the door-handle, as much to steady myself as anything else. I didn't seem to be able to move my legs properly. My hand didn't seem to be working either.

Just as I flicked off the lock, Bunny must have pulled from the outside. My hand seemed to explode, and I think I must have screamed.

Anyway, there I was lying on the pavement on my back, looking up the skirt of a very tall Qantas air hostess, who was looking down at me in equal amazement.

Of all the opportunities I'd had for a good chat-up line, simply croaking 'Hospital' wasn't one of my best.

Still, you can't win 'em all.

One or two now and then would be nice, though.

Bunny drove. I sat in the back with Rayleen (couldn't you have guessed?), and she made me put my right hand in her lap while she ran her fingertips over most of the rest of my body looking for other injuries. If my right hand hadn't felt as if somebody had grafted a bunch of bananas onto it and then dipped it in acid, it would have been a pleasant experience. Rayleen didn't find anything else broken, though she seemed convinced I'd been run over by a steamroller.

Bunny kept talking as he drove, but I had no idea what he was saying. I didn't really have much idea of what was going on at all. I remember seeing lots of traffic lights, mostly red ones, zip by, and then the lights of Goodge Street underground station, some of which were still working.

Then we were staggering into a hospital casualty department, and I was grateful Bunny was there – they can be dangerous places on a Friday night. Rayleen helped too, or rather her uniform did, giving us a pseudo-official status that meant we could jump the queue. The fact that she could swear like a trooper and at one point told a nurse that I was a security guard escaping from a hijack attempt, also helped.

I was lucky, of course. They always say that if they think you've been in a fight, although it was still short of chucking-out time.

A harassed young intern assisted by a cool, pretty nurse (called Ruth, from Stanmore) told me that I was bucking the statistical trend by having three fingers smashed between the knuckle and the phalangeal joint. He told me that the central finger always goes first, followed by the ring finger and then, if you're lucky, the index. The little finger usually escapes, as mine had. And there had been no damage to any arteries; the small amount of blood there was had come from minor cuts from the broken bottle.

The intern cleaned me up, then made me lie on a trolley in a curtained cubicle. The nurse (just 22 and looking forward to her holiday in Greece) checked my hand for bits of glass and then applied an impression splint. That would come off in two days, she told me, and be replaced by a spatula splint, and yes, she would be on duty on Sunday.

She'd given me a shot to kill the pain, and it was making me drowsy. I asked if I could see the people who'd brought me in, and after a few minutes, Bunny and Rayleen appeared at the bedside.

'What time is it?' I asked. 'Oh, and thanks for the lift.'

'Going on 11.00, and don't mention it, it was your diesel,' said Bunny cheerfully.

'I had a bag in the cab,' I said, thinking it was important.

'I know, I was driving the both of you,' quipped Bunny, doing a quick Groucho Marx walk around the bed. Rayleen looked at him as if he'd dropped from behind peeling wallpaper.

Bunny straightened up and took my wallet out of his back pocket. He flipped it on my chest.

'There's no cash left, you've been caned. No watch either, if you were wondering.'

That was nice of Nevil. He'd provided me with a cover story – I was supposed to look as if I'd been mugged. Then again, I had. Two hundred travelling money plus two hundred in bad rent money, a watch, my building society account book, three hours of my life and a few digital bones. Well and truly mugged.

'They left the tapes in Armstrong, that's one thing,' said Bunny. 'Oh – and they didn't take your swimming trunks either.'

'Who's Armstrong?' asked Rayleen, reasonably enough.

'The taxi we came in,' answered Bunny honestly.

'Why was he wearing swimming trunks?'

'The sunroof leaks, you wombat. How should I know?'

'I thought you said he was a friend.'

'He is. I drove him here, didn't I?'

Rayleen raised her eyebrows to the heavens and reached into her clutch bag for a pack of cigarettes.

'Not in here, I'm afraid.' It was the intern again, this time holding a clipboard and looking official. 'I've got some questions for you, if you're up to them.'

'I'd really like a smoke first,' I croaked, laying it on with a trowel.

'Entrance hall, if you really must. I'll be back.'

I swung my legs off the trolley and sat up. My hand throbbed, and with the quickly-drying plaster, it looked like an Indian club sticking out from my shirt sleeve.

With my left hand I fumbled inside my wallet. My driving licences were still there and the odd bits of paper you always accumulate. The card with Malpass's phone number was still there.

'Jacket?' I asked vaguely.

'We left it in the car,' said Rayleen.

'Armstrong's keys were in the pocket,' said Bunny.

'Good. Let's go have a smoke.'

It's still the easiest way to get thrown out of hospital. In fact, the three of us, all with duty-free Marlboros well alight, were shown the door in no uncertain terms. Once outside, I threw my cigarette away.

'Where's Armstrong?'

'Round the corner in the space marked Consultant Gynaecologist.'

'Thanks. Want a lift somewhere?'

'Nah, that's okay.' Bunny put an arm round Rayleen's waist. 'We'll get a minicab. They're cheaper.'

'And more reliable,' I said.

'You can't let him go off like that,' hissed Rayleen loudly. Then she made a fist under Bunny's chin. 'And don't give me any crap about a man's gotta do what a man's gotta do. The only thing a man's *got* to do in this world is stand up when he pees.'

Bunny had found a philosopher. They were in for an interesting night.

'You're right, Rayleen,' I said. 'He can't let me go – until he gives me my keys.'

'Oh, sure,' said Bunny, fumbling in his pocket.

'And a couple of quid; I've got the munchies.'

Bunny handed over a fiver, and as I walked away I heard him whisper to Rayleen.

'He's hungry. That's a bad sign.'

It took me ages to work out how to get Armstrong's door open, but thank God the ignition is on the left. It then took the rest of the century to get my leather jacket on over the plaster. I was shivering and sweating at the same time. I wasn't fit to drive. 'I'm not fit to drive,' I told myself. I was repeating myself as well.

By using my right knee to steady the wheel when I changed gear, I managed to get Armstrong out of the hospital car park. I was tempted to call it a day there and then, pull over and have a kip, but my stomach reminded me that I hadn't thrown it a bone since the ploughman's at lunchtime, and it had been quite an eventful day.

There was a fried chicken place open on Baker Street; about the only thing that was. It wasn't a Kentucky Fried, more a Bayswater Sauté, but it had seats, and the two black guys on duty in the bright red uniforms were so bored they took no notice of me. I ordered a double portion of chicken and a 7-Up and went to a table while they went back to the late movie on Channel 4 on a portable television.

The chicken came in a box, and the plastic cutlery, salt, pepper and freshen-up tissue all came in sealed envelopes designed for people with two hands. I opened them with my teeth and found that most had more flavour than the chicken.

It wasn't a good place to sit and sort out your future. I sat and looked at my reflection and that of the formica table in the window.

Outside, Baker Street was closed down for the weekend except for the Barracuda Club, which had taken over from the original School Dinners restaurant after it moved across the road to usurp the No 34 Wine Bar. It was good to think that life's rich pageantry continued even on Baker Street, a much neglected London thoroughfare remembered only by devotees of Sherlock Holmes (now the Abbey National) and Gerry Rafferty (who probably banks there).

I made a decision, or rather I hedged my bets.

I would ring Malpass. If he was there, I'd tell him about Nevil and what had happened. And where Jack Scamp was hiding out. That ought to be enough to bargain myself clear of the whole mess.

Oh yes, I knew where he was, even though I'd been unconscious going in and coming out, because I'd been there before. In fact, I'd suspected before tonight. Dead wise after the event, that's me.

If he wasn't home, I'd go back to the squat and keep my head down for a few days. Well, at least until Sunday, when I was on a promise at the hospital with Ruth and some new bandages. By that time, I guessed, Scamp would have got clear. After all, he wasn't packing suitcases for fun.

Suitcases. Abroad. French francs. I'd seen a 100-franc note on the mantelpiece at old

Ma Scamp's place. Scamp was planning a bunk to France. My, but I was sharp. I wondered if Malpass had any vacancies.

I found a phone box and dialled his number. That was my first mistake.

He answered, and I said who I was. That was my second.

How many are you allowed?

CHAPTER FOURTEEN

Malpass told me to meet him in Bateman Street. I wasn't too keen – there would still be plenty of punters wandering about even at one o'clock in the morning. ('Do you know what the fucking time is?' – 'No, Jack Scamp's stolen my watch.' That had got his attention.)

Was I sure he was hiding in the back room of the Mimosa?

Are frogs waterproof? Of course I was. I knew an empty beer keg when I was tied to one, and the last time I'd seen that particular one there had been a young punk called Emma sitting on it nostrilling certain noxious and probably illegal substances.

Was I sure it was Scamp? No, it was Lord Lucan in drag. Could I describe him? Yes. He's the only person I know who looks like his passport photograph, and he breaks people's hands. Oh yeah, that's him.

I said I had no intention of being within a couple of light years of the Mimosa when Plod and the SWAT team burst in. Malpass said I had a pretty clear-cut choice. I could either meet him near there or he'd have me picked up as a material witness and see how

I enjoyed sharing a cell with Jack Scamp. That seemed to me to be a fairly convincing argument, and I was too tired to put up much of a fight.

Soho was quieter than I'd thought it would be. A light rain shower had hurried the last of the rubber-neck tourists off the streets, and the restaurants and sex shows (mostly on video these days) were switching off their come-hither lights. There would still be a bit of clublife here and there through the alleyways, and the all-night gambling schools in Chinatown, though those were usually reserved for the Oriental abacus-for-brains fanatic. But on the whole, Soho was quiet enough for choir practice these days.

I parked Armstrong half on the pavement on Bateman Street, a cut-through little road running west-east, whereas most of Soho is north-south, with a pub on each corner and new shiny offices where once there were honest porn merchants and working girls plying their trade.

I felt oddly naked without my watch; I always do. It's an affectation I have. Another one is getting myself into situations and then wondering what the hell I was doing there. I decided to give Malpass another five minutes and then I'd disappear. When I thought five minutes were up, I decided to give him another five. I had nothing else planned for the evening.

Oddly enough, I didn't feel nervous. Not then, anyway. I had moved the rubber-handled wrench from the right side of the driver's seat to the left, but I knew its reassurance was mostly psychological. I could never get a decent swing with my left hand, but at best I would use it only to repel boarders. I had no intention of leaving Armstrong, and had kept the engine ticking over, as there was no way I could start him up in a hurry.

I had killed the lights, and my night vision was well adjusted when he arrived. He almost ruined it by parking right up behind me and flashing his headlights once. He made sure I knew it was him by flicking on his interior light and waving me towards him. There was no sign of any other cars or tanks or armoured personnel carriers and no indication that the police Stukas were waiting to come in and bomb the last pockets of resistance.

Malpass's car was a five-year-old Vauxhall that had seen better days, but then haven't we all. The interior was still waiting for its first clean, and the upholstery felt as if it had been textured in buff nicotine.

I sat in the passenger seat and nursed my plaster cast. Malpass looked at it and offered me a cigarette and then a light.

'You look like you've had a right trousering,' he said succinctly.

'Nicely put,' I said, and drew on the cigarette until it made me light-headed.

'How did you find him?'

'He found me.' And I told him what had happened.

'You were lucky, considering you were set up,' he said philosophically.

'You reckon?'

'Don't you? You're not thick. Do you really think Nevil was just out for a stroll when he saw your cab? The wife must have guessed it was you and tipped him off. She's used you before, to get her stuff back, to establish an alibi for when Jack was going over the wall. Why not again?'

'But why? Just to get me off her back?'

'No, to keep Jack happy. He's been out for nearly a week. Why do you think he's still around? He's been waiting to get even with you, that's all. She probably decided it was best to get it over and done with, and then Jack could finally skip town.'

I was speechless, but my brain must have been ticking loudly.

'Didn't think she could do a thing like that? Not to you?' He shook his head slowly. 'You should spend less time contemplating your navel and more time studying human nature, sonny. Like me.'

Sonny again.

'Well, you have more spare time on your hands, Mr Malpass.' It was a cheap shot but the only one I could come up with.

'Where do you think he's headed?' I asked.

'Boulogne, almost certainly.'

'Why Boulogne?' But it explained the 100-franc note I'd seen at Ma Scamp's and, come to think of it, the wad of francs I'd spotted in Bill Stubbly's wallet when I met him in the bank. Was it only yesterday? Well, it was the day before yesterday by now.

'It's the only place he's ever been outside this country. In fact, it's one of the few places he's ever been outside London. He used to go regular with his ma when he was a nipper. His dad's buried there, you see.'

'What was wrong with Woolwich Crematorium?'

'It probably wasn't working in May 1940. Jack Scamp senior was killed just before Dunkirk. Young Jack was born in early '41 and never knew him. Brought up by his ma right from the start.'

'That maybe explains a lot,' I said, reaching for another cigarette.

'Explains perhaps, but knowing why he turned out a wrong 'un doesn't make it easier to forgive and forget.'

'You really hate him, don't you?'

Malpass looked away.

'Like nothing else on earth, young Angel, but I don't expect you to understand. Unless the likes of Jack Scamp are put away for good, law and order will never have any credibility. He laughs at us, the courts, the judges. He just doesn't care what he does or who he hurts. You should know that. No remorse, not a shred of guilty feeling. If he hasn't already killed somebody, then it's only a matter of time. He's known as Mad Jack inside, you know.'

'I can see why,' I said sourly. 'So, where's the big manhunt, then? Why haven't we seen wanted posters up for this dangerous loony now he's on the run?'

'Priorities.'

'Yeah, Jo said that.'

'What?'

'She said you didn't have the manpower to watch them round the clock.'

Malpass made a snorting sound.

'She's laughing at us too, but she's right. Scamp had done 13 months of a two-year stretch and he could've got out in a coupla months more if he'd kept his nose clean. So we get him back and he gets maybe an extra six months for going over the wall. Small stuff. He'll be out again this time next year.'

'If you get him back, that is.'

'Oh, I'll get him. If you're sure he's in the Mimosa, that is.'

'He is, or at least he was a few hours ago. He must have been hiding in the back room behind the stage all the time. That's why there's been no music on for a week.' It was also how he'd overheard me and Kenny the barman talking and drawn his own paranoid

259

conclusions, which had led to both me and Kenny wishing we'd taken out medical insurance.

'You reckon that this Stubbly guy is in with the Scamp mob?'

'I doubt it; probably just scared.'

I didn't tell Malpass about Stubbly's trip to the bank getting French currency, and I bet myself there had been more than the one I'd seen. But it did explain a lot, especially how Stubbly had managed to keep the Mimosa trouble-free over the years. He had influential friends.

'Well, we'll see about that,' Malpass threatened.

'What's the plan, then? Remember, I'm here under duress.'

'My bet is that Nevil has taken the girl already – maybe Dover to Folkestone. Or they could've got a plane to Paris; nobody would have stopped them. Jack'll go a different way. If they use a ferry, he'll go hovercraft. There'll probably be a car round here somewhere, waiting for him to pick up. He'll drive himself and leave just before dawn. Quietest time, you see. Won't get picked up as a suspected drunk-driver; he'll look like a rep getting an early start.'

'On a Saturday?' It took me a while to work out that it was now Saturday.

'Even better, go as a tourist, what the hell. You know as well as I do, everybody watches what comes into ports these days, not what goes out.'

Malpass put another cigarette in his mouth but didn't light it. He was looking ahead again, not focusing on anything particular.

My hand was throbbing, and light-headedness was giving way to a headache that made my left eyebrow twitch.

'Nobody's been past here for a good 15 minutes,' said Malpass suddenly. 'It seems quiet enough.'

'So what's the plan, Mr Malpass? Your plan, that is, not theirs.'

'You show me exactly where this place is and we wait for him to show. If he doesn't, we kick the door down.'

He reached into the back seat and picked up a briefcase, one of the old upright ones schoolmasters used to favour. He opened the clip, resting the case on his knees.

'Where do we meet the others?' I asked, feeling suddenly bilious.

'What others?'

Malpass removed a rubberised torch from the case, tested it once, then put it on the dashboard. Then he took out a black leather hip holster, and from that, a metallic-dull revolver with a barrel about three inches long. He broke the chamber, which opened sideways, and counted the bullets.

'I told you this was personal,' was all he said.

I could have screamed and kicked and refused to go. I could have threatened to hold my breath until I went blue. I could have called a policeman. I did the fourth most stupid thing; I went along with it.

'We'll take the cab,' ordered Malpass. 'Drive up and down a couple of times, check the area.'

Yes, sir.

I not only drove, I pointed out the darkened entrance to the Mimosa. I'd be a Special Constable before you could say 'fuzz.' Then I quartered the block and pointed out the fire exit, which was a battered red door in between a Greek restaurant and a graphic art studio.

'Is it ever used?'

'Never been known. The exit is by the Ladies and usually blocked with beer crates.'

'That's illegal,' said Malpass, but as he was in the back of Armstrong, I couldn't see if he was serious or not.

'Then slap the back of somebody else's legs,' I said. 'Not mine.'

I did two more lefts and then stopped about 30 yards down the street from the club. There were cars parked down both sides even if I'd wanted to get closer, which I didn't.

Armstrong ticked over. There was no other traffic, there were no other sounds. For a minute, I thought my luck had changed and something good had happened, like Malpass had had a heart attack and I had a corpse in the back.

'All right, this'll do.'

Bugger. The sod still breathed.

'Do for what, Mr Malpass?' What I'd really meant to say was: can I go home now?

'You stay here and keep the road blocked; nobody'll get past you. I'll go in and see if Jack's still there. If he comes quietly, I'll come out and signal.'

'And if he doesn't come quietly?'

'I reckon he will.'

I gripped Armstrong's wheel – not a totally impressive gesture with only one hand – and took a deep breath. Time to assert myself. Now or never; the situation was well out of control already.

'I want it understood, Mr Malpass,' I said as evenly as I could, 'that I'm not here.'

'That's okay, sonny, I hear what you're saying.'

(Rule of Life No 279: people who say, 'I hear what you're saying,' really mean they didn't want you to raise the subject in the first place.)

My mouth had gone very dry and my bladder seemed very full. None of these symptoms seemed to affect Malpass. He climbed out of Armstrong on my side and stood over me until I pushed down my window.

He had a black trench coat on and his right hand was deep inside the right pocket. In his left hand he held the torch.

'Just stay here until I come out. You'll keep the street blocked, and if you see any pedestrians wandering about, tell 'em to piss off. Once I'm out, you can disappear and we'll say no more about it.'

He wasn't looking at me as he spoke; his eyes were fixed on the tatty door of the Mimosa. He was breathing deeply and exhaling loudly. I wondered if John Wayne ever had to.

'What if Nevil shows up?' I had a bad thought. Then I had a worse one. 'What if he's in there?'

'No way.' Malpass shook his head but still concentrated on the faded yellow door. 'They wouldn't risk travelling together.'

'What if he's already skipped?' I was clutching at straws. 'What's to say he hasn't skipped already? I don't know he's still there.'

'He will be. He was always an early bird, was Jack. Did most of his naughties just before dawn. Early to bed, early to rise, early to steal, that's Jack. Human nature, you see. Study human nature.'

And with that he stepped across Armstrong's head-lights and walked towards the Mimosa, right hand in his pocket.

I hadn't asked him how he thought he was going to get in, and for one terrible minute I thought he was going to shoot the lock and kick the door in. No such dramatics. He produced what looked like a bunch of keys and very quickly had the door open, but he didn't go in immediately. He paused, looked up the street past Armstrong and went into a crouch.

He had seen something I should have, which was a car turning in from Soho Square and coming up behind me.

My right foot hovered over the accelerator pedal and I balanced Armstrong on the clutch. I wasn't as convinced as Malpass that Nevil was out of harm's way. Seeing him lying in a coffin with a stake through his heart might have gone some way to convince me.

The car drew up slowly behind me and stopped. I don't know what else I expected; after all, I was the one blocking the street.

From the shape of its lights, I guessed it was one of the small Peugeots. I relaxed a little. Surely Nevil couldn't fit in one of those?

The driver pipped his horn, almost apologetically. I couldn't blame him; nobody likes to pick an argument with a London cabbie. Then a posh voice came out of the window: 'What's going on?'

In my mirror I could see a woman in the

car as well. It was late and maybe she wanted to get home, or to a hotel, or maybe a car park.

I pulled my window down and twisted round so I could stick my head out.

'Geerrrahtoffit!' I yelled. 'Ain't you got eyes? Can't you see there's been an accident?'

The driver didn't need any prompting. He put the Peugeot into reverse and disappeared, one of the millions not wanting to get involved. Maybe Malpass had something about human nature after all.

When I looked back to the Mimosa there was no sign of him, but the door was open.

If I had any sense at all, I would have left then. Of course, if I'd really had any sense, I wouldn't have been there in the first place. But what proved conclusively that too many of the little grey cells had finally dissolved to mush was the fact that I still stayed there after I heard the shooting.

I knew what it was immediately. I suppose I'd half-expected it; seeing Malpass's pistol, the rest was almost auto-suggestion.

But even as I heard it, I knew it was not a revolver. Not that I'm any sort of expert, but I had misspent much of a happy youth in the 'Feeling lucky, punk?' school of cinema, and I could tell Clint Eastwood's Magnum from, say, the Magnificent Seven's Colt

.45s, blindfolded. (There was never any blood when people got shot in *The Magnificent Seven*. Ever noticed that?)

This was much more of a cannon type of thump, almost like a distant firecracker, and it was quickly followed by a second.

I pulled the window down again and stuck my head out. I felt I ought to call out to Malpass or maybe go and see if he was okay. On reflection, I decided to let him come to me. And as it turned out, staying inside Armstrong was just about the cleverest thing I did that night.

When Malpass did emerge, only a few seconds after the shots, it was dramatic enough to make me forget my churning stomach.

The door of the Mimosa was flung back and Malpass stood there framed in it. I thought for a moment he was gathering his coat tails around him, like a woman would gather a long skirt, but it wasn't that at all. He was clutching his right leg with both hands, and that was how he tried to run across the street, like some rubber-legged Vaudeville comedian.

He yelled something as he ran/hobbled towards a parked sports car, but I just sat there hypnotised.

Then Jack Scamp appeared from inside the Mimosa, nattily dressed in white shirt, dark tie and dark blazer. He could have been anyone or anything stepping out after a night's wining and dining. Or course, the sawn-off shotgun he was reloading was a bit of a giveaway, though.

Malpass had made it across the street, about 80 feet or so in front of Armstrong. As he reached the parked sports car he went into a rolling dive, still clutching his leg, and bounced himself off the bonnet and over the other side. As he turned, the leg was straight up in the air, a position I'd only ever seen Springsteen get into voluntarily. Then he was gone from my field of vision, down behind the sports car.

He made it just in time, for Scamp had reloaded and fired again. Both barrels, I presumed, as there was only one crump, and the effect on the sports car was dramatic. Most of its soft top simply came away, but the whole car seemed to move sideways.

Scamp maybe said something to himself then, like 'Damn' or even 'Blast'; the sort of thing you would say to yourself when you'd just missed blowing a policeman's goolies off with an illegal weapon.

If Scamp did say something, I couldn't hear it. He just went about the business of reloading again, breaking open the shotgun and reaching into the pocket of his jacket for more shells.

I didn't know whether he'd killed Malpass, or whether he was taking it out on sports cars in general. I could relate to that; I mean, there's so little leg room in most of them. All I did know was that Scamp took a few steps forward into the street while stuffing home fresh cartridges. As he did so, he was directly in line with Armstrong's radiator.

At this point I did three things. First, and most importantly, I went out of my mind. Then I turned on Armstrong's headlights. Then I found first gear and stomped on the accelerator.

The design of the FX4 taxicab is about 30 years old now, and it was never really planned to make them more aerodynamic than, say, a brick at the best of times. In first gear from a standing start, on the level, they can't make more than about 15 miles an hour, and they scream a bit doing that. But they are heavy, and as fragile as a Centurion tank. Caught in the headlights, Scamp didn't turn a hair. He calmly snapped the sawn-off closed and swivelled it from the hip towards me.

Some people I know would revel in being able to say they looked straight down the barrel of a loaded gun. I can't, because I ducked down as low as I could, controlling Armstrong's wheel with just my left hand, the injured right tucked between my legs.

Oh yes, and I suppose I'd better come clean. I had my eyes shut.

I think I was probably screaming as well, but if I was, I didn't yell anything memorable. I heard the shotgun pellets hit the bonnet and the windscreen like hail-stones on a tin roof, and for a second I wondered if I should punch a hole in the glass like they do in the movies. But then I decided I had broken enough hands that night.

And then there was another sound that I didn't like to think about at all, but that I presumed was Jack Scamp hailing his last London cab.

I felt the nearside wheel go over something, and as there were no more shots, I opened my eyes. The street ahead was clear, so I slowed and risked a look in the mirror.

What was left of Jack Scamp was lying across the middle of the road, face down, about 50 feet behind me. I put my forehead on the steering-wheel and exhaled slowly. When I looked up into the mirror again, he was moving, crawling towards something behind him.

The bastard just didn't know when to quit, did he? So there was nothing else for it but Rule of Life No 4: never hit a man when he's down; run over him.

I put Armstrong into reverse and accelerated, driving just on the mirror. I have to admit that I felt a strange sense of elation as I hit him again; in fact I plumbed the depths of bad taste by yelling, 'Never one around when you want one, is there, Jack?' as Armstrong bounced for the second time.

After I turned the engine off and opened the door, I found my legs had turned to blancmange and moulded themselves into a sitting position. They had forgotten to tell the rest of my body about this, and as a result I slumped out of Armstrong, hitting the road with my right shoulder, having just remembered in time not to break my fall with my hand.

For a while, maybe a decade, I just hung there upside down.

Through the wheels of Armstrong, I could read the fly posters on a spare piece of wall on the other side of the street. I'd missed Meatloaf by over a year and Genesis's Invisible Touch tour was booked out. Life's like that sometimes; a real bitch.

Eventually I moved. I had to, as it's very difficult to throw up decently when you're upside down. In struggling upright, my face came level with the offside front wheel. Something wet and probably unspeakable was dripping from it.

I found my feet, staggered a couple of paces and spewed undigested fried chicken over a light-coloured VW Golf. I told you they get everywhere.

'Angel!'

Christ, he was still alive! Then I realised it was Malpass. He had levered himself up so that he was leaning on the boot of the sports

271

car Scamp had tried to demolish with his shotgun. The owner would not be well pleased. It had been an MG once.

Malpass was still clutching his leg, using his hands as a tourniquet. He was shaking, and his face was as white as a clown's.

'Did you do for the bastard?' he asked as I approached.

'You could say that. How about you?'

'I'll live.'

'But you'll never score at Wembley again,' I said, nodding at his leg.

'I've had worse. You look like death.'

'So does Scamp. I'd better get you some help.'

He cocked his head on one side. In the distance we heard a whoop-whoop siren.

'It's on its way, but you could phone in for an ambulance.'

'There's a phone in the club.' I looked across the road to the Mimosa. 'What happened in there?'

'The bastard was just leaving, I reckon. He was standing there with his bags packed. I think that horn tipped him off.'

The Peugeot that had come up behind me. 'A signal? Like someone was coming to pick him up?'

'Could be. You quite happy to let me bleed to death, then?'

'Hey, Mr Malpass, don't forget, I'm not here.'

'You might have trouble explaining that at the inquest, my lad.'

So that was the way the cookie was crumbling.

'And what about you doing your Wyatt Earp act without calling any back-up? Is that standard operating procedure?'

He narrowed his eyes and grimaced. Maybe he was in pain after all, a tough guy like him.

'Okay, we'll see what we can work out. But you'll have to get the gun for me. I dropped it somewhere near the door. Bloody Scamp had the sawn-off in a plastic dustbin. I thought it was his dirty washing.'

'Did he say anything?'

'Not a word. He saw me and started shooting.'

I could understand that.

'His reactions were like lightning, I'll give him that, but there was a table or something in the way, thank Christ. I never got a shot off.'

'Just as well, you'd only have annoyed him.'

The siren had gone. Why should we have assumed that a little thing like a gunfight in the street would attract attention?

'Go phone it in,' Malpass ordered, 'and stash the gun in the boot of my car. Then you piss off out of it and we'll say no more.'

'How will you explain Scamp?'

'Hit-and-run as he was chasing me. Nobody'll mourn him. I'll say I had an anonymous tip-off.'

'Seems reasonable.'

'Get a move on, then. Somebody's got to come along sometime.'

I agreed with that at least, and I was half-prepared to believe him when he said he could keep me out of it. I must have been in shock.

I shambled towards the Mimosa. What was hiding a bit of evidence compared to clubbing somebody to death with a black cab? No problem.

The only lighting in there came from a neon strip behind the bar. There was very little disruption; a couple of chairs were turned over and a table with most of its top scored off by shotgun pellets lay on its side. Bill Stubbly had got off lightly – so far.

I found Malpass's pistol and torch behind the table, and after a bit of contortion I managed to stuff them into my jacket pockets. On my way to the pay phone near the Gents, I noticed the door to the back room was open, and for some reason I decided to have a look.

I stepped over two zipper bags left in the middle of the small stage and reached around the door-jamb to fumble the light on.

There was the beer keg I'd been tied to, and the length of wire I'd probably been tied with lay on the floor. So did Nevil. He looked as if he'd taken both barrels into his chest at very close range. There was even a burn mark on his chin, but apart from that his expression was positively cherubic.

I didn't linger. Let Malpass figure it out. All I felt was relief that I could look over my shoulder now.

I went back into the club proper and headed for the phone. As I passed the Ladies, I noticed that the beer crates stashed in front of the fire exit had been moved aside. That gave me an idea.

One of the zipper bags on the stage was stuffed with French francs. I had no idea how much there was in there, but I reckoned it was probably what I was owed by the Scamp family plus a few expenses. I knew Malpass would have had no more than a fleeting glimpse of them, but just to be sure, I went behind the bar and found an empty crisp box.

I tipped about half the cash into the box and then took a couple of shirts from the second bag and laid them on top of the remaining cash. I was clumsy and had to pick up a couple of notes from the floor and wipe the bags where I'd touched them with a handkerchief. With only one hand, this seemed to take ages, and I hoped Malpass was a slow bleeder.

Folding the lid of the box together, I

hoisted it under my left arm and carried it to the fire exit. I had to put it on the floor to work the door-bar, and once I had it open, I slid it out with my foot. It blended in beautifully with the rubbish bags and empty bottles waiting for the refuse men, but with my luck they'd probably arrive before I could collect it.

As I was closing the door, I saw a car turn into the end of the street, very slowly and very quietly, driving on sidelights only.

It got closer, and I saw it was a dark-coloured BMW. I knew before I could see for sure that Jo would be driving.

The end to a perfect day, I don't think.

CHAPTER FIFTEEN

I did eventually phone for an ambulance, and even remembered to ask them to send the cops too, but not before I'd remembered to go through Scamp's other bag. I recovered my building society book, which was something, but I had to assume that my watch and sterling cash were somewhere about Scamp's person. The only trouble with that was that Scamp's person was somewhere all over the road.

Malpass had hobbled up the street a bit closer to the huddled mess, which I had no intention of looking at. He was still clutching his leg and his temper hadn't improved any. 'You took your bleeding time,' he snarled.

I thought I'd cheer him up.

'Hold the front page of the *Police Gazette* – Nevil's turned up his toes.'

'My God, but you're a dangerous bloke to be around. How?'

'Seems like Scamp decided to pay him off permanently. He's back there in the club. I don't think it happened much before we arrived.'

He looked down at Scamp again.

'Well, you're certainly helping the Met's clear-up rate. Did you get the gun?' I nodded and fumbled it out of my pocket.

'Not here, you berk, go and stick it in the boot of my car.'

We both heard a burst of siren that could have been either ambulance or the standard issue police Rover. They wouldn't use them all the way through empty streets at this time of night unless they were showing off.

Malpass took his right hand off his leg and fished out his car keys. I took them, and they were slippy with blood from his hand.

'Are you sure you're all right?' I asked, trying to sound concerned.

'I'll live, sonny. And I'll sleep better nights now. If you're going to do a runner, you'd better get moving.'

He was right. I handed over his torch so that he could flag down traffic or whatever policemen do at the scene of accidents and hurried round the corner to Bateman Street to sling the pistol into the boot of Malpass's Vauxhall. I took the precaution of wiping it with my handkerchief first, just in case the bugger had second thoughts and tried to plant it on me. I must have a suspicious mind.

Malpass was standing by Armstrong when I got back. We could hear engines now, coming down Oxford Street, but still no sign of any people, which was weird. I felt sure somebody must have seen us re-enacting the OK Corral, but in Soho after dark, a lot of people get suddenly short-sighted.

I gave Malpass his keys back and climbed aboard my trusty black steed. My head throbbed, but my right hand hardly hurt at all now. Maybe it had gone to sleep. I felt like joining it.

'You'll have to get this heap off the road while it's fixed, you know,' said Malpass, professional to the end.

'Yes, officer,' I said meekly. 'And I was never here.'

'Fair enough, I don't mind taking all the credit.'

'You're welcome.' I put Armstrong into reverse. 'One thing,' I said through the window.

'What?' There was another short burst of siren.

'How long had Scamp employed Nevil as a minder?'

'Not long. He recruited him while he was in the nick, we reckon. They shared a cell for a month or so in Wandsworth. Nevil got out around Christmas. Why?'

'Just curious. Did he have a second name?'

'Cooper. There's no family, if you're worried about somebody coming after you.'

'No, it's not that, just curious.'

I nodded to him and he nodded back and I reversed until I could turn into Soho

Square and then right into the parallel street to bring me to the Mimosa's fire exit. I kept the lights off, and as I turned, I saw the familiar blue flashes in the mirror that meant the cavalry had arrived and Malpass would be a hero.

I hadn't told him about the money, nor about the other item I'd found in Scamp's bag. But you can't have everything, can you?

If the ambulance had used its siren continuously, I'm sure it would have frightened Jo off. As it was, I was able to shove Armstrong's nose at 45 degrees across the bows of the BMW, and I scraped off a fair chunk of paintwork as I opened my door on to her wing. But I just didn't care any more.

She gawped when she saw it was me and froze until I knocked on her window with my splint. I could hear vehicle doors slamming in the next street. There wouldn't be much time before they searched the club.

Jo fumbled her hands beneath the steering-wheel and her window slid half-way down electrically.

'We can't go on meeting like this. No, correction: we just can't go on meeting.'

It wasn't one of my best, but not bad in the circumstances. The circumstances in particular included her pointing a small automatic pistol, business end first, at my chest. I'd seen so many guns that night I was beginning to think I was at a Belfast wedding.

'Where's Jack?' she said, with a twitch in her voice.

'There was a film called that, you know, about an 18th Century London highwayman. And then of course there was Jack Ketch, which is what they called the public hangman, after the real one who did the business for James II.'

'Stop gabbering. Where is he?'

'Okay, so I'm rambling, but it's all true, actually. I always rabbit on when people point things at me.'

She seemed to notice my splinted hand.

'I see you met him anyway,' she said coldly.

'Yeah, but we won't be going in for annual reunions. He's dead.'

I knew by then not to expect tears, but I did expect more than the flick of the head to take a strand of hair out of her eyes and a quick but loud sniff. Some people have no emotion.

'Did you kill him?'

'No,' I said. Armstrong was going to have to take the rap for that. 'The cops are here. At the front door. If you don't believe me, drive round the block and say hello.'

She stared straight ahead for a minute.

'They may come out of the exit there any second,' I said, praying they wouldn't.

Jo's gun disappeared. She must have had a

281

handbag on her knee.

'He killed Nevil, you know.'

'I thought he might.' Short of hitting her with a brick, I didn't think I was going to get a reaction out of her.

'Especially after you showed him this.'

I held up the thing I'd taken from Scamp's bag. It was a one-year British visitor's passport. It had Jo's photograph, but the name was Mrs Josephine Cooper.

'What did you do? Just let it slip that Nevil was planning on a double-cross?'

'Something like that.' If I'd expected her to try and grab the passport or throw a wobbler, I was disappointed.

'Was there anything between you two?'

'Nothing much. He was keener than I was.'

'How did he get you the passport?'

'There's a Civil Service strike on; don't you read the papers? All you need to get one of them is fill in a form at the post office and show some phoney identification. It's easy enough to get a provisional driving licence with a new name on it.'

Really, the deceit of some people. I wondered how long the strike would last, and what time the post offices opened on Mondays.

'So why get Jack out of nick?'

'He wanted out. His mother had been poisoning him during visiting hours, telling him I was carrying on. Jack couldn't stand it, but he never held it against me.'

'When it came down to it, you figured you'd be better off with Jack, so you dropped Nevil in it.'

She shrugged her shoulders. For her that was tantamount to visiting the Wailing Wall.

'Jack's the one with the money.'

'In Boulogne?' It was a shot in the dark.

'Yes. How did you know?' Surprise registered in her eyes. She was really running the whole gamut of her emotions now.

'How were you going to get there?'

'First hovercraft from Dover this morning. I have all my stuff in the back.'

She wasn't going to volunteer anything.

'How did he get the shotgun?' I was curious. Did she have the power to persuade Nevil to provide his own murder weapon?

'It must have been Bill Stubbly. He's been supplying Jack with bits and pieces since he got out.'

'What hold did Jack have over Stubbly?'

'He owned the club. Has done for a couple of years.'

That explained a lot and confirmed that everyone had known what had been going on except me. There was nothing more to be gained from talking to her.

'You can still make it,' I said.

'Make what?' She frowned.

'The ferry – the hovercraft – whatever. To

France, as the song says. Go for it.'

She gave me an up-from-under look, but only about quarter strength, so my legs didn't melt and my heart hardly fluttered.

Still cool as anything, she reached forward and started the engine.

'I'd get rid of the gun if I were you,' I advised, sensible as always.

'I will,' she said. Then she put her hands behind her neck and something came away in her fingers.

She held out her left hand through the half-open window. I put mine under it and she unclasped her fist. When I looked, I was holding the emerald pendant with the 'JJ' inscription.

'I don't want you to be out of pocket,' she said, 'and I won't be needing that any more.'

I slipped it into my jacket and climbed back into Armstrong to ease him back out of her way.

She didn't look at me as she drove off, and I waited until her tail lights had gone before I nipped out to recover the crisp box from the fire exit of the Mimosa.

I hate long goodbyes anyway.

I suppose I should have got Duncan the Drunken out of bed by throwing pebbles at his bedroom window and whistling softly, but where the hell do you find pebbles in Barking at 4.30 am? So I did the next best thing. I found a phone-box where the phone worked and the box didn't smell too badly of urine because the ventilation had been improved by somebody stealing the door. They've got a good sense of community in Barking. I rang Duncan's number and let the receiver hang loose. By the time I got through the last couple of streets, he'd be standing in the hallway swearing into his phone and just getting an earful of pip-pip-pip-pip sounds.

He was. I could hear the foul language from the doorstep, and when I rang the bell, he slammed the phone down with an audible crack.

'Hello, Duncan,' I said with a smile, 'you're up early.'

The smile wasn't difficult, despite what I'd been through. Duncan was wearing only tartan carpet slippers and a pair of Fred Flintstone boxer shorts. It would have made a Jehovah's Witness smirk.

'Angel.' Duncan scratched his stomach. 'What in buggery are you doing here at this time?'

'Just passing, Duncan, and I saw your light on. I need some help.'

'Oh aye? Well, it's lucky I was up, wasn't it? Bring yourself in and put the kettle on. I'll go and tell Doreen not to fret.'

'Who is it, Duncan?' yelled Doreen from upstairs.

'That daft pillock Angel, honeybun. You go back to sleep.'

Honeybun? Well it seemed to reassure her; she was snoring loudly before the kettle whistled.

Duncan pulled on a pair of overalls and straddled a kitchen chair while I served him his tea.

'You've hurt yer hand,' he said, like other people say it's raining.

'It's a hard life out there, Dunc.'

I sipped some tea and burnt my lips. I was more convinced than ever that Duncan had an asbestos mouth.

'You in bother, then?'

'No,' I said fairly truthfully, 'I think I've just got out of it, but I need a bit of help covering my tracks.'

'Oh aye?' that was a bad sign; he was thinking about it.

'I don't want money,' I said hastily, and he relaxed visibly. He was a Yorkshireman, after all. 'I need a motor for a few days.'

'What sort?' Duncan the professional.

'Anything with four wheels and a tax disc.'

'For how long?' Duncan the very professional.

'Until you've repaired Armstrong.'

He considered this, then stood up and put his mug in the sink.

'Better have a look, then.'

Outside, he ran a wise old hand over Armstrong's radiator and bonnet. Then he put his hands on his hips and narrowed his eyes at me. There was the first gleam of a dirty dawn in the sky, but Duncan could size up a motor blindfold at night.

'Been grouse-shooting, have we?'

'I thought that was illegal before the twelfth of August.'

Duncan scratched his head.

'Well, I don't reckon there's owt here that Doreen can't put right.'

'Doreen?'

'Aye. Didn't I tell you she was doing panel beating at night school?'

How on earth could that have slipped my mind?

'Well, to be honest, Duncan, I hadn't thought of Doreen using Armstrong as homework.'

'It'll be right, lad. I'll guarantee all the work and respray him meself.'

Well, that was something, though Duncan's famous three-hour parts and labour guarantees were not worth the bits of paper they were scribbled on. But I was too tired to argue.

'What about a stand-in? And please, not that Kraut Transit again.'

Duncan smiled. 'Got a good price for that the other day. No, I've just the thing for you, but I'll have to charge you.'

'How much?'

'A ton, on condition you keep the mileage below five hundred a week.'

'A ton a week? You franchising for Hertz these days?'

'But wait till you see what I have in mind.'

I let Duncan drive Armstrong round to his lock-up and open the doors. Armstrong would be out of sight and out of mind of any curious policeman there, unless of course Duncan got raided, which wasn't beyond the bounds of possibilities. But then it would take a pretty tough policeman to con-front Doreen in full panel-beating swing.

Inside the lock-up was an ancient Morris Minor badly in need of repair, but worth its weight in rust to collectors these days.

Duncan saw my face as he got out of Armstrong.

'No, not that – that.'

He pointed to his left, and I turned my aching head and then immediately cheered up at the sight of a bright red Mercedes 190; what some people call the 'baby Merc' but in Hampstead is known as 'the second Merc.'

I clapped Duncan on the shoulder with my good hand.

'Duncan, it's perfect.'

What the hell, I could afford it. And it would make Frank and Salome furious.

Frank was furious all right, but more

because I made him come down from the top floor in Stuart Street and open the front door. I thought that was a bit of a selfish attitude, as he would have been up at 6.30 anyway showing off his new jogging Nikes. Or was it the Reeboks this week? I lose track.

I'd driven the Merc very gingerly. After Armstrong, it was the difference between surgery with a laser and amputation with a chainsaw. But I made it somehow, parked right behind Frank's and Salome's Golf and staggered to the door clutching my bag and the crisp box. At that point, I'd more or less given up. The legs had gone rubbery and the brain was like chocolate fudge cake. I knew I had some keys somewhere, but couldn't work out where, and I didn't seem to have a spare hand.

I leant my forehead on the doorbell and heard it ring. I was sure it would be Frank who answered. Lisabeth would be deep in the Land of Nod, Fenella still had her parents with her and nobody ever saw Mr Goodson at the weekend.

'Yes?' Frank started. 'What...? Good God, man, you're as white as a sheet!'

'You're not, Frank,' I beamed, then fell into his arms.

We wrestled for a while as he tried to pick me up. He had the strength to do it easily, but I was a bit bulky and uncooperative as I refused to let go of my bag and crisp box.

He finally got me in a sort of fireman's lift and then proceeded up three flights of stairs. He was in shape, I had to give him that. And so, I was happy to notice, was Salome. Wonderful shape, in fact; or what was showing through the split-front shortie camisole, which was only just decent in three places.

I gave her one of my charmer smiles – I've got good teeth; so show 'em, that's what I say – but I think it came out more of a leer. Anyway, she took a step back as Frank propped me in a chair.

'Angel, darling, you look like death,' she said.

'Don't soft-soap me, Sal, give it to me straight.' I waved my splint at her. The bandages were filthy. I must have resembled a mummy from a cheap horror flick. 'Do me a favour, just let me kip for a bit.'

'What's wrong with your place?' asked Frank, breathing deeply, his black, muscular chest heaving with the etc.

'Lisabeth.'

'Oh,' they said together.

'When she's up, just roll me downstairs, okay? Don't ask anything till about Tuesday, huh?'

Salome looked at Frank and shrugged in a 'why not?' sort of way.

'One thing,' said Frank, hitching up his pyjama trousers (the trendy traditional sort). 'Is that your car outside?'

'Sure,' I said, looking at Salome. 'I thought I should change my image to keep up with the DINKS.'

He looked puzzled.

'Double-Income-No-Kids,' Salome explained, then said to me: 'I always preferred SWELL.'

'So do I,' I said. Then I fell asleep, leaving her to tell Frank about Single-Women-Earning-Lots-in-London.

Lisabeth and Fenella gave me a hero's welcome back to my flat when I surfaced around one o'clock.

Fenella's parents had been seen off back to Rye earlier that morning, so there was general cause for rejoicing, and Lisabeth was already moving back to the marital home.

'We think it was awfully sweet of you not to wake Lisabeth this morning,' said Fenella. 'She needs her sleep.'

'It looks like you had a good party,' said Lisabeth sternly.

'Party?' I was only just awake and looking for somewhere to stash the crisp box before anyone asked me what was in it.

'In Plymouth, wasn't it?'

'Oh yeah, great, great. But it got a bit out of hand.' I showed her my splint. 'Out of hand. Geddit?'

'I won't ask how you did that,' she said

reprovingly. 'But I will make you lunch.' She clapped her hands together. 'How's that? As a welcome home.'

'Er ... fine. Poached eggs on toast with Marmite.' Not even Lisabeth could ruin that, could she?

'Does Marmite have meat in it?' she said suspiciously.

'No, it's yeast extract.'

'Well, okay then.' She sounded dubious. Maybe she had forgotten the recipe.

'But first I need a complete MOT,' I said, motioning for Fenella to help me off with my jacket.

'What's that?' asked Fenella.

'A complete MOT of the person – shit, shower and shave.' She giggled and blushed from the neck up. 'And I might need somebody to soap my back. I'm not sure I can manage with only one hand.'

'Binky! Come and help crack these eggs this minute!'

Home sweet home.

I took the crisp box into the bathroom with me and turned the shower on. While it was warming up, I peeled off my clothes and then, stark naked, I riffled through the box.

I hadn't read a *Financial Times* lately, but by my crude arithmetic I had close on eight thousand quid in francs. I could always go and ask Salome; she'd know the exchange rate. But then I decided I'd better have a shower and put some clothes on first. Frank wasn't that broadminded.

Despite some black looks from Lisabeth, I sat down to lunch wearing only a towel. Lisabeth's poached eggs could have doubled as squash balls, but I was hungry enough not to mind, and it was fun having Fenella lean over me to cut them up for me and butter extra toast.

They shared the washing up and then left for their own pad, offering an invite to dinner that night. I declined, thinking they'd probably rather be alone.

I think Lisabeth felt that too.

At the door, Fenella turned and asked if 'that rather natty red car' outside was mine, and I said it was.

'Where's Armstrong?' she quizzed.

'On holiday.'

'So what do you call this one?'

'I was thinking of Bormann maybe, but I'm not sure yet. Fancy a spin in him?'

She opened her mouth in an excited Oooh, but before she could say anything, Lisabeth's podgy hand gripped her shoulder and she was yanked out of the room.

As I dressed, I turned the radio on to BBC Radio London. It's the best station for London news; a pity nobody listens to it. There was nothing about dead bodies or homicidal taxis in Soho. So far, so good.

I opened up Brogan's *History of the USA* and replaced my building society book, driving licence and passport, which Nevil had left in the bottom of my bag. I couldn't get all the francs in there; they'd have to stay in the crisp box for the time being. But some of them would have to go straight away, as I was right out of folding money. I even owed Bunny a fiver, although for picking me out of the gutter, so to speak, I owed him a lot more. Maybe I'd get him a present.

I stuffed about a thousand francs into my pocket and retrieved the JJ pendant from my leather jacket. My personal bureau de change and pawnbrokerage wouldn't ask too many questions, and it was open all day Saturday.

Mr Cohen's Exotic Pets was only just round the corner, so I decided to walk. Taking the Merc – and letting Mr Cohen see it – would also insure a lousy rate of exchange.

I thought at first that the Merc had got a parking ticket, but it wasn't, it was a printed fly-sheet stuffed under the wiper blades. It read: THIS CAR IS A SYMBOL OF SOCIAL DIVISON – YUPPIES OUT! CLASS WAR LTD.

Bloody cheek. The amount they cost, they ought to be socially divisive. I didn't know who Class War Ltd were, but it was a good name for a band. I replaced the leaflet under the rear windscreen wiper of Frank's Golf.

There weren't many exotic pets on show

in Mr Cohen's emporium: a macaw and a parrot and the usual collection of hamsters, rabbits and small unidentified furries. But then it wasn't as if selling pets was Mr Cohen's main source of income. He dabbled. In this and in that. Mostly that, if money was the bottom line.

I'd often meant to ask him why he bothered with the pet shop front, as most of the animals seemed to give him asthma. I'd also meant to pluck up the courage and one day ask him why he was called Rajiv Cohen, but not today, as there was business to be done.

Mr Cohen looked over the top of his half-rims at me when I asked him if he'd like to buy some francs.

'Just come back from holiday, have we?'

'You could say that, Mr Cohen.'

He produced one of the new currency calculators that all the whizzkids in the City have clipped to their identity bracelets, and began punching buttons.

'The rate is 9.62 to the pound. I can give you 6.50.'

'That's some commission, Mr Cohen, but I'll take a thousand's worth, because I want your advice on something else.'

'Oh yes? And what would that be?' he asked as he counted out 65 quid in fivers in exchange for my wad of thin, brown French notes.

I dropped the pendant on the counter in

front of him, and as if by magic a jeweller's eyeglass appeared in his eye. I'll swear his hands hadn't moved.

'Of course the inscription devalues it,' he started, establishing the right bargaining atmosphere. 'But it's a nice stone, I'll give you that.'

'I'm told it's worth over three grand, Mr Cohen,' I lied.

'Well, I don't know about that, son, but I can ask my brother in Brick Lane. He's the gems man of the family.'

Over Mr Cohen's shoulder, I could see into the back room of the shop, and through the window there I spotted Springsteen jumping up on to the fence. Once balanced there, he looked over his shoulder to check that the coast was clear. It must be a family trait.

In his mouth was a white, furry creature. Maybe it was a coming-home present for me.

I kept Mr Cohen arguing and haggling for a good five minutes before agreeing to leave the pendant with him until Monday. Well, I had to give Springsteen enough time to get clear. He'd do the same for me.

Stan at the off-licence looked pleased to see me, even though I interrupted him checking his pools coupon against the football results on the radio. I ordered a couple of packs of

Red Stripe Crucial Brew and a bottle of Bull's Blood, a real headbanger of a Hungarian red wine, and forty Gold Flake.

'Another party tonight, Roy?'

'No way, Stan. Feet up, telly on. That's Plan A for tonight.'

He raised an eyebrow in surprise.

'Anything good on the box?'

'Probably not, but after this little lot, it won't matter.'

He nodded wisely.

'Still, it's a pity you're not going to a fancy dress do. You could've put a glove on and gone as Michael Jackson.'

He was still chuckling as I left. In another era, Stan would have been the one in the air raid shelter who tried to keep everybody's spirits up during the Blitz. No wonder the Luftwaffe had a go at East London.

On the way back to Stuart Street, I worked out my menu for the evening. I had some steaks in the freezer compartment of my fridge and I could scrounge some garlic from Salome and some potatoes from Lisabeth. A hefty chunk of protein, a glass or three of wine, maybe a good book, and then ten hours' solid kip. That should just about set me up for my return visit to the hospital, and I was trying to remember what time Ruth had said she went on duty on Sundays, so I hardly noticed the Renault 5 parked behind my new Merc.

I had another life and death struggle with the lock of No 9, but managed to get the door open without dropping anything or damaging my right hand.

'Here he is,' I heard Lisabeth say.

She was sitting on the stairs next to a very attractive, curly redhead who was showing long lengths of red, diamond-pattern stocking between a pair of red-and-black high heels and a short, red-leather mini. Across the mini-skirt lay Springsteen, on his back, allowing the redhead to tickle his chest. He opened one eye at me as if to say, 'Now get out of this.'

'Hello,' said the redhead, 'I'm Tracie Boatman.'

Oh knickers.

'Tracie's been after you for days, Angel,' said Lisabeth primly. 'So I'll leave you two together.'

For once, I wished she wouldn't go, but I put a brave face on it.

'Yeah ... er ... sorry. I did get your messages but ... er ... I've been busy. You'd better come up to the office.' I nodded towards my flat.

She stood up, and Springsteen, the rat, went limp with an audible sigh and allowed her to carry him up the stairs like an over-indulged Roman emperor. I wondered what he'd done with the hamster or whatever it was.

'I didn't know the National Insurance office worked Saturdays,' I said resignedly.

'Oh, we don't.' She smiled. 'In fact, we try not to work Monday to Friday. Can I give you a hand? Oh, I'm sorry, I didn't mean that. What on earth have you been doing to yourself?'

'Road accident,' I said bravely. 'Pulling an old man out from under a bus.'

'Really? What a hero.' She looked as if she believed me about as much as Springsteen did.

'Can you get the keys out of my pocket, please?'

I swivelled my right hip towards her and, without batting an eyelid, she dug deep into my trousers. If she was going to do me for non-payment of National Insurance, then I was going to get my money's worth.

She let us into the flat, and Springsteen jumped out of her arms and scampered into the bedroom. If he'd left his present in the bed, he was dead meat.

I dropped my shopping in the kitchenette, she plonked herself on the sofa.

'So, what can I do for you, Mrs Boatman?'

'It's Ms actually, I'm divorced.'

You know when you're getting old; the divorcees look younger.

'I understand you put bands together,' she said, looking round the flat.

'Yes,' I said slowly. 'Usually just for friends

who want to play together.'

'Can you get me a trad jazz band for next Thursday?'

Was this a trick question? 'Where?'

'A pub called the Chiswell Street Vaults. Do you know it?'

'Yes.' It was the sort of pub you left only when you needed a change of clothes. 'What's the event?'

'A hen party for one of the Inspectors in our office. She gets married next Saturday and we want to give her a good send-off. We've hired the back bar for a party and we need some music and we know she's a jazz fan.'

'We?'

'Oh, there are about 40 of us. It's a big office.'

Forty women on a hen night in a pub I knew was good value. Mmm.

'I'm sure I can do something, Ms Boatman.'

'Call me Tracie. Do you mind if I smoke? So many people don't these days.'

'Not at all,' I said, and remembered the cigarettes I'd bought. 'Try one of these.'

'Oh, I like them,' she said greedily. 'They're good and strong.'

Mmmm.

'What would a band cost?'

'Well, I may be out of it,' I said, holding up my hand. 'But I can easily get a drummer, pianist – if there's a piano there – bass man, and of course you'll need a sax player.'

That was Bunny's debt paid off.

'Maybe 80 quid plus a few beers. How's that sound?'

'Fine. We might even have enough left in the kitty for a kissogram, you know, a Tarzanogram or similar. The girls like to let their hair down.'

I slipped a Eurythmics tape into the stereo.

'I might be able to help you there as well,' I said. And that would put me in Simon the Stripping Sexton's good books. He never turned down work.

'Fancy a drink? I was just going to have one.'

'It's a bit early,' she said half-convincingly.

'Well, the truth is, I might need some help with the corkscrew.'

'Oh, of course, your poor hand. Where is it? Do let me help.'

This splint could come in useful, I thought.

I brought the wine and a pair of glasses through from the kitchen. She'd slipped off her jacket and had curled her legs under her. Her eyes widened when she saw the bottle.

'Bull's Blood! I haven't had that since I was at university.' She set to it with a will and the corkscrew.

I popped back into the kitchen and took two steaks out of the freezer, putting them in the oven out of Springsteen's way.

'You know something?' I asked gaily. 'I felt sure your visit was a professional one.'

She smiled and poured the wine.

'You behind on your NI stamps, then? Don't worry.' She winked an eye. 'Your cat didn't grass on you. And anyway, this isn't my area. You must be naturally lucky,' she said, laying it on a bit.

'Yeah, I think I am. I always say I am; it's my Rule of Life Number One.'

She raised her glass in a toast, then slipped off her shoes and recurled her legs under her.

'What is?'

'It's better to be lucky than good.'

The publishers hope that this book has given you enjoyable reading. Large Print Books are especially designed to be as easy to see and hold as possible. If you wish a complete list of our books please ask at your local library or write directly to:

Magna Large Print Books
Magna House, Long Preston,
Skipton, North Yorkshire.
BD23 4ND

This Large Print Book, for people
who cannot read normal print,
is published under the auspices of

THE ULVERSCROFT FOUNDATION